S0-AGQ-291

Books by Michael Lister

(John Jordan Novels)
Power in the Blood
Blood of the Lamb
Flesh and Blood
The Body and the Blood
Blood Sacrifice
Rivers to Blood
Innocent Blood
Blood Money
Blood Moon
Blood Cries
Blood Oath
Blood Work

(Cataclysmos)
Cataclysmos Book 1
Cataclysmos Book 2

(Remington James Novels)
Double Exposure
Separation Anxiety

(Merrick McKnight Novels)
Thunder Beach
A Certain Retribution

(Jimmy "Soldier" Riley Novels)
The Big Goodbye
The Big Beyond
The Big Hello
The Big Bout
The Big Blast

(Sam Michaels and Daniel Davis Series)
Burnt Offerings
Separation Anxiety
Blood Oath

BLOOD Work

a John Jordan Mystery

Book 12

by Michael Lister

Pulpwood Press
Panama City, FL

Copyright © 2017 by Michael Lister

All rights reserved. No part of this book may be reproduced in any form or by any means, electronic or mechanical, including photocopying, recording, or by any information storage and retrieval system, without permission in writing from the publisher.

This is a work of fiction. Any similarities to people or places, living or dead, is purely coincidental.

Inquiries should be addressed to:
Pulpwood Press
P.O. Box 35038
Panama City, FL 32412

Lister, Michael.
Blood Work / Michael
Lister.
-----1st ed.
p. cm.

ISBN: 978-1-888146-70-7 Hardcover
ISBN: 978-1-888146-69-1 Paperback

Book Design by Adam Ake

Printed in the United States

1 3 5 7 9 10 8 6 4 2

First Edition

For

The victims and their families
and
the law enforcement officers who
ensured there weren't more of them.

Thank You

Dawn Lister, Jill Mueller, Mike Harrison, Terry Lewis, Aaron Bearden, Tim Flanagan, and Lou Columbus.

Chapter One

Before being arrested, tried, convicted, and ultimately executed by the state of Florida, Ted Bundy, perhaps the most notorious serial killer in American history, cut a bloody swath across my part of the Panhandle.

It began at dawn on Sunday, January 8, 1978, when Theodore Robert Bundy arrived at the Trailways bus station in Tallahassee and began to blend in among the tens of thousands of college students returning for the spring semester.

After only a week in Florida's capitol city, in the early morning hours of January 15th, shrouded by dark of night, Ted Bundy entered the Chi Omega sorority house at Florida State University through a rear door with a faulty lock.

In less than fifteen minutes, and within earshot of some thirty potential witnesses, he viciously assaulted four young coeds.

Sometime around two forty-five in the morning, he bludgeoned Margaret Bowman with a piece of oak firewood while she slept, after which he garroted her with a pair of nylon stockings.

Moments later, he stole into Lisa Levy's bedroom

and beat her unconscious, strangled her, tore one of her nipples nearly off, bit her so deeply in her left buttocks that it left his bite mark impression, and sexually assaulted her with a hairspray bottle.

A few moments after that, he entered the adjoining bedroom occupied by Kathy Kleiner and broke her jaw and deeply lacerated her shoulder.

A short while later, he snuck into Karen Chandler's room and brutally assaulted her, knocking her teeth out, breaking her jaw, crushing her finger, and leaving her with a concussion.

In less time than it takes water to boil, Ted Bundy savagely attacked four young women inside the Chi Omega sorority house, murdering two of them, but he wasn't finished yet.

Eight blocks away, Bundy broke into a basement apartment and attacked another FSU student, Cheryl Thomas, dislocating her shoulder and fracturing her jaw and skull in five places, leaving her with permanent deafness and an equilibrium complication that ended her dance career.

On February 8th, Bundy stole an FSU van and drove east on I-10 to Jacksonville, where he unsuccessfully attempted to get fourteen-year-old Leslie Ann Parmenter into the van with him.

On February 9th, in Lake City on his way back to Tallahassee, Bundy abducted twelve-year-old Kimberly Diane Leach from Lake City Junior High School.

On February 12th, Bundy stole yet another car and left Tallahassee, heading west on I-10 across our part of the Panhandle for Pensacola.

On February 15th at one in the morning, Bundy was

pulled over by Pensacola police officer David Lee after the Volkswagen Beetle he was driving came back stolen in a wants and warrants check.

This is what we know of what Ted Bundy did, but what about what we don't know?

Before his execution in Florida's electric chair in 1989, Bundy confessed to killing some thirty women in seven states, but in a recently released memoir, Bundy's former attorney, John Henry Browne, revealed Bundy confided in him that it was more than three times that.

Did Ted Bundy kill over one hundred women?

If so, when? And where? And who?

What did he do, who did he attack and kill between arriving in Tallahassee on January 8th and the slaughter at Chi Omega on January 15th?

Who did he murder and rape between his attack of Cheryl Thomas on January 15th and his abduction of Kimberly Diane Leach on February 9th?

Who did he brutalize and butcher between leaving Tallahassee on February 12th and his arrest near Pensacola on February 15th?

Could Ted Bundy be responsible for the disappearance of Janet Leigh Lester near Marianna in the early morning hours of February 12th following her Valentine's Day Sweethearts' Ball, as he made his way west on I-10?

Could he be the monster responsible for the open, unsolved case that devastated an entire town, utterly shattered two families, and still haunts Jack Jordan, my dad and the man who many believe let the killer get away?

Chapter Two

Anna and I are making love when the call arrives.

The *buzz buzz* of my phone on the nightstand in our dim, hushed bedroom illuminates a small area around it and joins our breathing and intimate expressions as the loudest sounds in the room.

"Get it if you need to," Anna whispers. "I'm not going anywhere."

I shake my head. "Absolutely not."

Our first attempt at making love this evening had been interrupted by Taylor's upset little cries coming from the baby monitor on Anna's nightstand, and we had only recently returned to this secret sacred sanctuary where we alone worship.

"What if it's—"

I glance at the number being displayed.

"It's not Johanna," I say. "Everyone else can wait."

As an investigator with the Gulf County Sheriff's Department and a chaplain at Gulf Correctional Institution, I get a lot of emergency calls. But it's as the dad of a young daughter who lives with her mother much of the time that I most often check my phone before the first vibration is concluded.

"But—" she begins.

"Homicide, kidnapping, hostage situation, riot . . . doesn't matter."

She smiles up at me. "Thank you."

It's August in Florida and hot even inside our air-conditioned home with a fan and window unit running, and a small bead of sweat rolls down my nose and drops onto her forehead before I can catch it.

"Sorry," I say, and ineffectively attempt to wipe my face on my bare shoulder.

"Don't be. Clearly I adore your body fluids and I love it when our sweat mixes."

"But you're not sweating," I say.

"Only because you're doing all the work. We can flip around if you want me to sweat on you."

The incessant buzzing on the hard surface of the bedside table has a certain relentless rhythm to it.

"Did you start . . ." Anna begins. "Are you moving in sync with the vibrations of the phone?"

"Not consciously," I say with a smile, "but I think maybe I am."

She laughs that laugh that lightens the world.

Our lovemaking is many things—sometimes playful, others intense, sometimes gentle, others aggressive, sometimes sacred, others profane. At times we talk and laugh our way through the early stages of our entanglements. At others the only noises able to escape our mouths are unintelligible expressions of ecstasy and private words whispered from passion-hoarse voices.

This evening our lovemaking is tender, nurturing, restorative.

When my phone stops vibrating, I return the full
weight and focus of my attention to the woman I have
been in love with since we were kids, casting aside all
thoughts of the call, who it might be, what they might
need.

Being intimate with Anna is my favorite thing in all
the wide world, and everything else I feel and experience
while one with her is infused with gratitude.

Looking down at her bottomless brown eyes, I feel
as if I could dive right into them and never resurface, and
in a very real way that's exactly what I'm doing.

"Some women go their entire lives without ever being looked at the way you look at me," she says.

"Some go their entire lives without having sex to the
rhythm of a vibrating cellphone," I say.

"If they're lucky, neither group knows what they're
missing," she says.

Our eyes lock again.

She had confided in me near the beginning of our
relationship how much she loves our intense eye contact
while we make love and that Chris, her ex, would never
look at her, would never open the windows to his soul
while in the vulnerable state of sexual intimacy.

My phone vibrates again to notify me whoever called
left a voicemail message, but it's as desultory as the swish-
ing, swirling sound the little window unit and box fan are
making.

"Who was it?" Anna asks. "Who doesn't know how to
leave a tender moment alone?"

We are lying on the bed, our moist, naked bodies

entangled, all the covers shoved down toward the bottom.

I am holding my phone above us, squinting to see who had called and caught us *in flagrante delicto.*

"Don't recognize the number," I say.

Without moving my torso, which her head is partially propped on, I reach over and replace the phone on the nightstand.

"What're you—you're not gonna check the message?" she says.

"Eventually," I say. "I'm busy right now."

I put my other arm around her and pull her even closer.

"Now, come closer and whisper secrets to me and let's keep the outside world away for just a little longer."

She does and we do and for a short, inviolable while, there is no world outside this one.

And when I do finally listen to the message, I wish we had kept it at bay even longer.

The call had been from a bartender at 22, the Package and Lounge out on Highway 22. The message, "Come and get your brother before I make an official call to the cops."

Chapter Three

I open the door to the newly remodeled little bar wondering how many I've been in over the years.

Dim and nigh quiet.

Smoke and chatter and laughter and Chris Stapleton's version of "Tennessee Whiskey" playing softly on the jukebox.

"Oh hell," Jake yells from the far end of the bar, "it's on now."

The large, sullen man sitting next to him with thick, sunbaked arms and hands looks up from his drink. I have no idea what he's drinking because the rather large glass is completely obscured by the massive mitt of his right hand.

"My alcoholic brother is in the house," Jake adds. "This round's on me. Whatcha drinkin', John? 'Bout some Tennessee whiskey?"

I cross the dance floor, nodding at the two middle-aged men shooting pool in the small side room, feeling an old familiar familial dread that dates back to childhood.

The wooden bar is in a squared U-shape with people

seated on three sides. When I reach this end of the bar, a young brunette Sunday-night bartender is waiting for me.

Behind her on the back wall, the rope lights on the mirrored shelves of whiskey change colors, and something about the bright, beautifully colored bottles and the way they're displayed makes me think of Christmas.

"He's out of money and he keeps demanding drinks and he won't give me his keys," she says. "I'm new and I didn't know what to do. Bonnie said call you."

I glance over her shoulder at Bonnie, a pale elderly lady with poofy bottle-black hair stacked high on her head nursing a glass of white wine.

Thank you, I mouth to Bonnie.

She lifts her glass and nods toward me.

"You did good. Thank you for calling me. Figure out what we owe and give Bonnie a glass of wine on me."

"Thank you."

She moves down the bar toward the register and her pad, and I make my way over to where Jake is slumped on his stool.

On the wall behind Jake is an enormous red and white neon Budweiser sign with a lit crown above it. Seen from a certain angle it looks like the crown is sitting atop Jake's head.

As I move over toward Jake, he starts shaking his head. "John, John, John. Never 'spected to see you here. But it's okay, buddy. I won' let you 'rink too much. I promise."

"What're you doin' in town?" I ask.

"Visitin' Dad."

Since retiring, our dad has spent far more time at his fishing cabin here in Wewa than at his home in Pottersville.

"He's over here most of the time these days," Jake says, "and I still see him more than you do. It's like you don't even care."

Though Dad had been of retirement age, retiring hadn't been his idea. He lost the election that would have kept him as the sheriff of Potter County for yet another term. When he did, Jake, a deputy in Dad's department, lost his job too.

Both men have had difficulty adjusting to their new reality, but some eight months later, Dad has found a certain equilibrium investigating unsolved homicide cases he always meant to return to, while Jake is still lost. Unemployed. Perhaps unemployable. He's tried a few different things but nothing for very long.

"Come on," I say, "we'll go see him now."

"You go ahead. I'm gonna . . . I'm gonna stay . . . and have another 'rink or two. This place is so nice now. I really like what they've done with the place. Isn't this place nice? I like it here. Do you like it here? What am I saying . . . you like all bars, don't you, big brother?"

"It's nice, but it's time to go."

The beefy man beside him looks up from his drink and glares at me. "He says he wants to stay and have a drink. Hell, let him stay and have a drink. He ain't botherin' nobody."

"I ain't botherin' nobody," Jake says.

"Tennessee Whiskey" ends and "Smokin' and Drinkin'" begins.

From across the bar, beneath a huge blue neon Bud Light sign, Bonnie says, "Go with your brother, Jake. We'll be here tomorrow night. Come back then."

Jake's face clouds over and he looks wounded as he

20

tries to focus on her.

The thick man beside Jake looks over at me again. "You here as a cop or his brother?"

"Why?"

"Determines how involved I get."

"Whichever one gets you the least involved," I say. "Come on, Jake. Don't make this difficult."

"One more drink," Jake says. "Have a drink with me. Just one. Just one more. Then we'll go check on Dad."

"You need to go with him, Jake," the bartender says.

"You need to calm your tits, Leslie Jean," he says.

"I ain't servin' you another drop, so you might as well go with him."

She then lets me know how much the bill is and I pay it, tipping her well.

"Buy me one and I'll help you get him to the car," the big man beside him says.

Jake whips around toward the man and falls off his barstool, laughing as he lands on the floor as if it's the funniest thing ever.

Far quicker than I would have thought him capable, the huge man jumps off his own barstool, bends over, and pulls Jake from the floor to his feet in one smooth motion.

Now that he's standing, I can see that the thick man is even bigger than I realized. Not only does he tower over us, but one of his arms is larger than both of mine together.

"Thanks," I say.

"Time to go, partner," he says to Jake.

"One more drink," Jake says.

"Not tonight, brother. Let's go."

Without waiting for Jake's consent, he lifts him by

21

the arm and walks him toward the door.

"You're a good friend, Goliath," Jake says to him as they pass me.

I lay a twenty on the bar. "For Goliath's next several drinks. And tip yourself well out of it too."

Chapter Four

"You really got your shit together," Jake is saying. "And I really respect that. I do. You don't drink anymore. You don't. You've got a family. Smokin' hot wife. She is. I hope you don't mind me sayin', but she is. You know? Two beautiful girls. They are. Both beautiful in their own way. You really got it together, big brother."

We are winding down Lake Grove Road in a low-slung fog toward Dad's little cabin on the Dead Lakes.

It's a damp, dark night and the rural road that dead-ends into the Apalachicola River is desolate, only the narrow swath of headlights providing any illumination at all—and it's mostly the reflective bounce back of the fog.

High humidity and everything is moist. Wipers on intermediate, clearing occasionally the droplets of dew clinging to and sliding across the windshield.

"I've never had my shit together," Jake is saying. "Not really. Not totally. But used to be a fuck of a lot better than it is now. Now, I'm a wreck. A train wreck. A . . . interstate pileup. A . . . a mess. I keep tryin' to get it together, but . . . I . . . just can't. Ever felt like that? Like the ends of whatever you're tryin' to grab are like that goddamn fog out there and you can't pull them together. You try. Truly you do. But they won't . . . you can't get a hold of them."

Foolishly, I start to respond, but realize he's not pausing for a response, only taking a quick breath.

"I need a damn job," he says. "That's what I need. Hey . . . Hey . . . you know what? You know what? You could get me on with the sheriff's department over here. I could be a deputy here. We could work together. How about that, man? Wouldn't that be cool?"

I have been dreading this moment for as long as I've been working at the Gulf County Sheriff's Department, and am glad it's drunk Jake who's asking, and hope he won't remember it tomorrow.

"'Course now with Dad needin' me, I ain't really got time to work no way, but I need to. You know? A man needs to work in this world. He does. I do. You got two jobs . . . I ain't even got one."

"What does Dad need you for?" I ask. "You helpin' him with his investigation?"

"Oh, that. No. Not that bullshit. That's some foolish-ass shit. He ain't gonna solve that case after all this time. He's only tryin' 'cause he ain't got nothin' better to do and he's thinking about legacy and shit. If he was gonna solve it, he would have solved it back then. Not thirty-something years later. You know? That girl's gone. Gone baby gone. She ain't never gonna be found. What would they find anyway? A bunch of old bones? Who needs that?"

Her mother, I think. *Our father.* And countless other people who carry her vanishing around with them like their own stalking specter.

"I don't know," he says. "Maybe I should help him. Hell, I ain't got anything else to do. 'Cept drink. Do too much of that I might end up like Mom. Do you miss her? I don't really miss her, John. Not really. Am I a bad person? Am I? I just . . . We were never close, you know? And God, I thought she was so weak, so . . . I don't know. I just—"

A deer grazing on the side of the road darts out of the hot, dark dampness and I slam on the brakes.

I hadn't seen it until we were already upon it. There was little time to react.

The car skids, sliding on the damp pavement, the driver's side above the headlight and the front quarter panel striking the poor creature.

"Oh fuck," Jake says. "What was that? What did you hit?"

"A deer. You okay?"

"Yeah. Yeah, I guess. Just startled the piss out of me. Shit man. I didn't know what was . . . Is it dead?"

"I'm gonna check. Stay here. I'll be right back."

I shove the car into Park, pull up the emergency brake, turn on my flashers and my emergency lights, and get out.

The sheer level of its volume always startling, the cacophony of nocturnal noises coming from the river swamp on both sides of the road is as discordant as it is deafening.

We're between two curves in a dangerous spot, even with my lights splashing across the moisture-laden tree branches and dark pavement.

I've got to hurry.

Across the opposite lane and about five feet into the ditch, the animal lies unmoving except for labored breaths and moans of pain.

A good-sized doe, the gentle, beautiful creature is

not long for this world. All I can do is shorten her suffering.

Squatting down beside her, I withdraw my weapon.

"I'm sorry about this, girl," I say. "All of it."

I then press the barrel to her forehead and squeeze the trigger.

The rapport is deafening, reverberating around me, bouncing off the thick forests on both sides of the road, momentarily silencing the crickets and frogs and other nocturnal noisemakers.

Standing, I reholster my weapon, check for traffic in both directions, and rush back over to the car, withdrawing my phone as I do.

Inside the car, I call a local farm family with several children who could really use the meat from the deer that will otherwise go to waste.

Jake starts talking again, but I ask him to give me just a second.

When Stevie answers his phone I say, "It's John Jordan. Sorry to call this late. I've just hit a deer on Lake Grove Road and had to put it down. I hate for the meat to go to waste but I can't do anything with it. Thought you might want it."

The moment I pause, Jake starts trying to talk again, but I hold up my hand.

I laugh as Stevie asks me if this is part of some sort of sting operation I'm running with the game wardens.

"I swear to you it's not," I say. "It'd be entrapment if it were, but it's not. You want it or should I call somebody else?"

When he tells me he wants it, I let him know where it is and disconnect the call.

"Damn, John," Jake says. "Why didn't you let me or one of my friends get it? You know I ain't got no job right now. I could've eaten venison steaks and stew for a month or more."

Trying to change the subject, I say, "What does Dad need you for if not the investigation?"

"Whatta you mean? Just stuff. Taking care of him. Helping him do the stuff he's too weak or tired or whatever to do."

"Like what?" I ask. "What's he too weak to do?"

"Huh? Not much now, but soon it'll be lots of stuff."

"I don't understand. Because he's getting older?"

"What? No. Because he's sick. He ain't told you? That's why he's tryin' to solve this damn case so hard. Wants to do it before he dies."

Chapter Five

I find Dad asleep in an old recliner I'd swear he had when I was a child—the one I'd climb up in with him to watch *Columbo* or *McMillan & Wife*, the sweet smell of his pipe swirling around us.

Trying not to wake him, I ease past him, quietly half carrying Jake down the short hallway to the spare bedroom.

Jake, in a stupor now, is no longer talking, but his breathing, moans, and awkward movements are loud and I figure it's only a matter of moments until he wakes up Dad.

Glancing back over my shoulder, I can see Dad has yet to even stir.

The cabin is small, rustic and creaky, and looks and smells like only men live here.

Very much a camp, a temporary getaway, this crude, tiny shack is not suited to serve as a permanent residence, but that's exactly what it has become for these two men on extended retreat from their lives.

When we reach the spare bedroom and I click on the large, old light switch, I'm surprised but not shocked by what I see.

All the furniture, including the bed, has been removed, and the space has been converted into a homicide investigation war room.

The walls are covered with maps and pictures and notes and suspects and images of evidence—all from the Janet Leigh Lester case.

In the center of the room, a single folding chair sits at a single folding table with the murder book and various papers and file folders atop it. Directly next to the murder book on the right side is an open composition book with a blue pen on it, Dad's small, neat handwriting partially filling the page beneath the pen.

Jake opens his eyes and lifts his head slightly long enough to utter a single-syllable word. "Couch."

I help him back down the hallway and onto the old slip-covered couch not far from where Dad is asleep in his chair.

Standing upright again, I look down at the two hurting and lost men—one at the middle of his life, the other nearing the end—and consider their plight. Neither has a job or relationship. Their lives are largely devoid of structure, purpose, and meaning—Jake's perhaps more than Dad's, especially if Dad's thrown himself into the Janet Leigh Lester case to the extent it looks like he has—and both men in different and similar ways are adrift.

Dad lets out a small snore, coughs, turns his head a little, and readjusts his body in the chair.

Is he really sick? Dying?

It hasn't been long since we lost our mother. Are we about to lose our father too?

I have never been as close to my dad as I would have liked. He's a decent man with lots of friends and the respect of many, but all of his friends are social, casual, of the shallow acquaintance type.

I have far fewer friends, but our connection is much more intimate, personal, deeper.

As good and stable and mostly supportive as Dad has been, he's always kept me, like everyone in his life as far as I know, a certain distance away. At our closest, we have never been truly close. In those most intimate of moments over the course of our lifetime as father and son, I still felt like they weren't nearly as intimate as they might have been.

My relationship with my dad has always felt like we were on different sides of the glass partition of a penitentiary visiting booth, a barely visible barrier between us, communicating through plastic telephone receivers. Nothing direct. Nothing too personal.

Like so many men I know, and not an insubstantial number of women, my father seems completely uncomfortable with vulnerability—his own or anyone else's. This leads to a certain opaqueness and impenetrability of character that makes relating difficult and true intimacy impossible.

Every time I think of this, I'm reminded of what Rumi, the thirteenth-century Persian poet and Sufi mystic said. *The wound is the place where the light enters you.*

Without wound, without openness, without vulnerability there is no place for exchange—of light or anything else.

For much of my life, I tried to change the nature of our relating and communicating, something that kept me continually frustrated. Later in life, I found peace through letting go of what I wanted and accepting what is.

Am I about to lose even that?

Deciding not to wake him, I make my way over to the door, feeling excitement and gratitude at being able to crawl into bed next to Anna when I get home.

Easing open the door, I step through it and quietly close it behind me.

I head down the wooden stairs and into the front yard toward my car, but I don't get very far.

Pulling out my phone, I call Anna.

Still readjusting to marriage and family life, I try to remember to let Anna know where I am and what I'm doing as often as I can, especially given the deception and violation she was subjected to in her previous relationship.

"Hey," she says, her voice soft and sleepy.

I tell her everything that's happened and what Jake said about Dad dying.

"Oh John, I'm so sorry. Do you think there's something to it or was it just drunken Jake-isms?"

"Not sure."

"Do you need to stay and talk to him?"

"You know that case he's been asking for my help with?"

"Bundy?"

"I feel like I need to stay and look over it. Do you mind?"

"I'd rather have you here in bed with me," she says.

Anna is so strong and resilient, I have to remind myself how much she has been through lately. Following the disintegration of her marriage to Chris and learning about all the ways in which he had betrayed her, which were staggering in both breadth and depth, she had experienced extreme physical and psychological trauma while pregnant. She is still healing, still recovering, and I need to be mindful of that at all times.

"And that's where I'd rather be, but if Dad *is* dying I feel bad for telling him no."

"I understand, and if he was awake and you were spending time with him it'd be different, but . . . Do what you need to, I just really rather you not be tired tomorrow," she says.

Tomorrow we are meant to be meeting her folks at a rented cottage on Mexico Beach for our first vacation as a family and my first vacation in—well, maybe my first ever as an adult.

"Thought the whole point of going on vacation was to rest and relax."

"Okay. But . . . I'm just really lookin' forward to this, to getting away together."

"I know you are," I say.

"And I know you're not," she says. "I just keep thinking somethin's gonna come up and you're gonna back out."

I'm not good at getting away, at vacations, and she knows it. It's not that I don't like, enjoy, and need downtime or family time or time alone with Anna. I do. I adore those things. And my approach is to incorporate them into our lives—day in and day out, integrating relaxation and cele-bration into our ordinary lives, not just during a one-week getaway each year. But I also know it's important and help-ful to actually go to a different location occasionally, and even more important than that, I know how much it means to her, so I'm not going to back out on her tomorrow—no matter what.

"I won't let it," I say. "I promise."

"Thank you."

"If you really don't want me staying and taking a look at the book, I'll—"

"No, it's okay."

"You sure?"

"Yeah."

"Really?"

"Really. Now go get to work."

"I'll be in bed beside you before you know it."

Chapter Six

What is it about cold cases?

No matter how old or cold they are. People are still obsessed with solving the Jack the Ripper, the Black Dahlia, and the Zodiac cases. Two decades later, when little Jon-Benét Ramsey would be an adult woman in her midtwenties, millions of people are still fascinated, intrigued, even obsessed by her case.

But that's nothing compared to the utter obsession experienced by the cops who worked the case that went cold.

Why do we become so utterly obsessed with unsolveds?

I'm still actively working both the Atlanta Child Murders and the Stone Cold Killer cases. Decades later and I'm still haunted by them, plagued with solving them.

Unsolved homicides are like demons that can only be exorcised in one way by the cops who worked them. You can solve them and be free, or fail to and remain possessed by them for the rest of your days.

I think of the cold case files on my desk right now. One, the Remington James case, involving the death of several men and one young woman in the river swamp near the other end of Cutoff Island. The other, a series of cops killed with their own guns, one of whom was our current sheriff and my boss Reggie Summer's predecessor.

I don't know how many cases haunt my dad—maybe it's just the ones related to Bundy's time in the Panhandle or maybe there are others I know nothing of—but now that he's nearing the end of his life, I understand why he wants to put to rest these ghosts. How much more so, how much more urgent, if he's sick or dying?

On Valentine's Day in 1978, while I was obsessed with getting Anna to dance with me at our school's Valentine's Day ball, my dad, Jack Jordan, was obsessed with finding Ted Bundy.

Of course, he didn't know it was Ted Bundy at the time. He didn't even know he was looking for the same killer in both instances. He only knew he was working two particularly brutal and bloody cases—the Chi Omega Killer in Tallahassee and the Broken Heart Butcher in Marianna.

Valentine's Day that year was supposed to be the day when Kimberly Diane Leach got to wear her new blue dress to a Valentine's Day dance of her own in Lakeland, Florida, but on February 9th, the day her parents were going to take her to buy her that blue dress, she went missing from her school in Lake City.

This was a full two years before I would become obsessed with another serial killer, the Atlanta Child Murderer, and I never realized it until now but I learned obsession from my dad.

My obsession with Wayne Williams and the Atlanta Child Murders was in a way a shadow, an investigative echo of my dad's obsession with Ted Bundy and with the Janet Leigh Lester case.

Pulling the big blue binder of the murder book toward me and flipping to the first page, I look up at the walls covered in case notes. I remember a similar room from a much earlier time.

I still recall Dad coming to my room to talk to me about my grades and how he and Mom thought I should come to live with him for a while, and the look on his face when he saw that my room was covered, much the way this one is, with all the witness statements and police reports and pictures of evidence and crime scene photographs I could get my hands on.

Removing the pen from the blue college-ruled Yoobi composition book, I turn the pages back to the front.

Before I even begin, I do two things—do a quick and cursory review of Ted Bundy on my phone, and make a list of questions I want answered.

One of the most organized, efficient, and sophisticated serial killers to ever operate in the United States, Ted Bundy was a predator unlike any our nation has ever known.

Considered charismatic and handsome by many of his young victims, when Ted Bundy was operating at his horrific best, he would approach young women in public places, either pretending to have an injury or disability or impersonating a law enforcement officer or other authority figure, later overpowering them in or near his car and taking them to a preplanned secluded location for assaults that included rape, sodomy, bludgeoning, strangling, and sometimes even decapitation and necrophilia.

Theodore Robert Bundy was actually born Theodore Robert Cowell. He was born to Eleanor Louise Cowell at

Elizabeth Lund Home for unwed mothers in Burlington, Vermont, on November 24, 1946. Though an air force veteran named Lloyd Marshall is listed as the father on Bundy's birth certificate, the actual identity of his biological father has always been in question. At some point later in life, Ted's mother claimed that she had been seduced by a sailor named Jack Worthington, but no records of anyone with that name in either the navy or merchant marines has ever been found.

There are those in Bundy's family who believed that Louise Cowell's own father Samuel Cowell, a violent, abusive man, may have actually been Bundy's biological father.

For the first few years of Bundy's life, he lived with his maternal grandparents, Samuel and Eleanor Cowell, and actually believed they were his parents and that his mother, Louise, was his sister.

In 1951, Louise met Johnny Culpepper Bundy, a cook, at an adult singles night at the First Methodist Church in Tacoma, Washington. When they married later that year, he adopted Ted.

Though Bundy often lied about his early life, he confessed to more than one interviewer and biographer that as a young person he roamed his neighborhood, searching through trash cans and dumpsters for pictures of naked women and detective magazines, crime novels, and any lurid material involving sexual violence, especially ones that involved pictures. Consuming large quantities of alcohol, he also stalked young women, peaking through draped windows to observe them undressing and engaged in other private personal activities.

After graduating high school in 1965, Bundy attended the University of Puget Sound for one year before transferring to the University of Washington. In 1967, he met and became romantically involved with one of his classmates, Stephanie Brooks (not her real name), who later broke things off with Ted and returned to California, fed up with what she described as Bundy's lack of ambition and immaturity. A critical turning point in his demented development, Bundy was devastated. There is little doubt that Brooks served as a type for Bundy's victims, who were by and large white females from middle-class backgrounds between ages fifteen and twenty-five, mostly college students who had long dark hair parted in the center. He evidently didn't approach anyone he'd ever met before. Eventually Ted would reunite with Stephanie Brooks and later become engaged to her for the express purpose of rejecting her the way she had him.

After his relationship ended with Stephanie Brooks, Ted worked a series of minimum-wage jobs and volunteered at the Seattle office of Nelson Rockefeller's presidential campaign. In August 1968, he attended the Republican National Convention in Miami as a Rockefeller delegate. In 1970, he reenrolled at the University of Washington as a psychology major. He became an honor student with a good reputation among his professors. In 1971, he took a job at Seattle's suicide hotline crisis center, working alongside Ann Rule, a former Seattle police officer and aspiring writer, who would later write a book about Ted titled "The Stranger Beside Me." Ironically, during the time they worked together, Ted, who Rule described as kind, solicitous, and empathetic, would actually walk Rule to her car at the end of her shift each night to ensure her safety.

After graduating from the University of Washington in 1972, Ted became a rising star in the Republican Party, described as smart, aggressive, and a true believer. In 1973, Ted received a place and enrolled in UPS Law School in spite of a poor score on his admission test, but by 1974 he had begun skipping classes and eventually stopped attending altogether as young women began to disappear in the Pacific Northwest.

Over the next several years, Bundy would perfect his acumen as a predator and serial killer, abducting, raping, and killing young women in Washington, Oregon, Idaho, Utah, and Colorado.

Eventually, Bundy would be arrested and tried, but he escaped not once but twice, the second time bringing him to the Panhandle of Florida.

Smart, calculating, and unusually organized, Bundy used his extensive knowledge of law enforcement methodologies to elude authorities for quite an extended time.

He scattered his murders over large geographic areas, and had already killed well over twenty young women before various authorities realized they were hunting for the same man.

Meticulous and exacting, Bundy would explore his surroundings, searching for safe sites to dispose of his victims. His method of assault usually involved brutal blunt-force trauma and strangulation, which were far more quiet methods than firearms and left less evidence behind. Adept at minimizing evidence, he never left a single known fingerprint at any of the crime scenes nor any other evidence directly linking him to the crimes.

Bundy believed himself to be nearly invisible and in many ways he was. His generic, almost anonymous physical features gave him an uncanny ability to alter his appearance. A changeling. A chameleon. Nondescript. Invisible. He hid the distinctive dark mole on his neck by wearing sweaters and turtleneck shirts. Even his preferred vehicle, a Volkswagen Beetle, blended in like few cars could.

Bundy evolved as a sadist and serial killer over time, his organization and sophistication, his modus operandi, his hunting, his preying, his luring and trapping increasing in effectiveness and proficiency with each passing kill.

Eventually, Bundy would deteriorate, his sick and twisted psyche ultimately leading to his undoing, but before he began his descent, he was horrifyingly good at the very worst things a human being can be.

Having reacquainted myself with Bundy and his background, I remove a sheet of paper from the composition book and make my initial list of questions.

Who killed Janet Leigh Lester? How exactly was it done? When? Where? And where are her remains? Is it even possible that Ted Bundy did it? If so, where did the lines of their lives intersect? Even if it's possible, did he actually do it? If he didn't, who did? And how had the killer eluded apprehension all this time?

Questions formed, I dive into the murder book for the answers.

One of the things Harry Bosch taught me early on, something borne out in every experience I had had since—trust the book, the answers are inside.

The keys to solving the case lie within the murder book.

Chapter Seven

The old murder book is flimsy and falling apart, the blue vinyl covering the cardboard beneath splitting and peeling up.

Inside, the first deteriorating document is a typed case summary on a yellowing and brittle piece of paper.

The age and condition of the murder book and the evidence displayed in the room justifies Jake's derision and underscores the futile nature of such an endeavor—each only making me want to help Dad solve it all the more.

Just before I begin reading, I receive a text from Stevie letting me know he has retrieved the deer from Lake Grove and thanking me for letting him know it was there.

After winning the Miss Valentine pageant on Saturday night, February 11th, the newly crowned beauty queen, Janet Lester, and her boyfriend, Ben Tillman, attended the Sweethearts' Ball on Sunday night, February 12th, with their friends and classmates of Marianna High School.

Both events took place in the school's gymnasium.

Following the ball on Sunday night, Janet and her

friends hosted a party at an old farm-house in a pasture near a lake out on the desolate rural route of Highway 71. Witness statements vary widely on when Janet arrived at or left the party—or if she even came. Some of the kids report never having seen her there at all, while others claim she was there most of the night and didn't leave.

Early the following morning, when her stepdad, Ronnie Lester, got up for work and noticed she wasn't home, he began calling her friends, beginning with her boyfriend, Ben, and her best friend, Kathy. Both kids were asleep in bed and said they thought Janet was too.

Waking his wife and calling the police, Ronnie began to hunt for Janet, retracing her steps from the previous night as best he could, but a search of the school and farmhouse yielded no clues as to her whereabouts.

Later that morning, as Ted Bundy was attempting to pay for his breakfast at the Holiday Inn in Crestview with a stolen credit card with a woman's name on it, Janet's Mercury Monarch was discovered in an empty field off Highway 71 about halfway between the farm where the party had been and the I-10 exit where a man matching Bundy's description in an orange VW had gassed up late the night before.

The red Monarch, left to her by her grandmother who had passed away the previous year, looked eerie in the empty field as the sun streamed in behind it, but any exterior appearance of oddness of the abandoned boxy car in the vacant field paled in comparison to the horrors it held inside.

The entire interior of the car was covered in blood. Sprayed across the roof. Splattered across the windows. Smeared across the seats. The car dripped with blood. The passenger side floorboard held Janet's bloody tiara with strands of her blood-soaked hair in it, and there on the center of the front seat, a blood-drenched heart of Valentine candy lay ripped in half, its contents cascading out in a bloody chocolate broken-hearted mess on the seat.

It appeared that most of Janet's blood was in the car, but her body was nowhere to be found—and still hasn't been nearly four decades later.

From all accounts, Janet Leigh Lester was as beautiful within as she was without—and that's saying something.

I look up from the murder book to the enlarged yearbook picture of Janet tacked to the wall in front of the makeshift desk I'm seated at.

She had long, straight brown hair, parted in the center—just the way Bundy liked—big brown eyes, smooth skin with the slightest hint of a caramel complexion, and striking features, particularly her full lips, wide-mouth smile, and the depth and shape of her eyes.

She was genuinely good. Authentically kind. Consistently friendly. Popular with every segment of the population at Marianna High School.

She was a cheerleader, played volleyball, and was on the yearbook staff—this last because she was quite the photographer and planned on studying photojournalism in college.

Her high school sweetheart, Ben Tillman, had been her boyfriend since eighth grade, and her small circle of close friends were loyal and diverse.

Her best friend, Kathy Moore, said Janet was the single best person she had ever known, and the only possible motive for her murder was madness.

Her stepdad, Ronnie Lester, the only father she had ever known, owned a farm center and tractor supply place, where she worked part-time. He said she was the sweetest soul he'd ever encountered.

She helped her mother, Verna, who was somewhat sickly, with both the housework and taking care of her mentally and physically disabled little brother, Ralphie.

She was actively involved in both the Methodist church and 4-H, and treated Cinnamon Apple Ice Cream, her red-and-white-dappled Appaloosa, better than most parents do their children.

A handwritten note in the margin in Dad's small, neat print says, *I was doubtful at first that Janet was as good as everyone said she was, but I've come to believe she was even better.*

The first and most obvious suspect was her boyfriend, Ben Tillman, and he remains the prime suspect to many to this day.

The case was complicated because Ben was the son of Kenneth Tillman, the Jackson County sheriff at the time of the murder. Almost immediately, Sheriff Tillman, seeing the obvious conflict of interest with his department handling the case, called in his friend and fellow sheriff, Jack Jordan, to conduct the investigation.

For personal reasons—his distant cousin and goddaughter was a resident at Chi Omega at the time of the attacks—Sheriff Jordan was already involved in the case in Tallahassee, but gladly took the Jackson County case, having no idea when he did that he'd soon become convinced that the same killer was responsible for both.

Of course the first thing he did was look at Janet's

boyfriend, family, and friends, eventually clearing them all. He then looked at those who attended the farmhouse party that night and even Marianna's usual suspects, the little collection of career criminals in town—though none had ever before done anything like this, or anything that would indicate they could.

Ultimately, Dad had concluded that Ted Bundy killed Janet Lester, and had even attempted to get Bundy to confess to it and reveal the whereabouts of the remains, from the time he was arrested right up until his execution in Florida's electric chair in the early morning hours of January 24, 1989.

I know my dad. I have witnessed his integrity over many, many years. I know if he didn't think Ted Bundy killed Janet he wouldn't have said it. But he paid one hell of a price to do so, and it was believed by many both in town and regional, and in a few cases national, media who covered it, that he was only doing what so many had expected he would—cover up for his sheriff friend and his son, Ben, who they all believed to be guilty of the brutal murder of his kind, sweet, pretty girlfriend, Janet Leigh Lester.

Was I wrong? Dad had written on the first page of the composition book. *Did I let the murderer go free? Have there been other victims since then that I could have prevented? Is their blood on my hands? God, I want to find out before my time here is done.*

Chapter Eight

On Monday, January 2, 1978, both Ted Bundy and Janet Lester watched the Rose Bowl on TV—Ted in Ann Arbor, Michigan at a little local pub, after having escaped from jail in Colorado three days before, Janet on a large wooden cabinet console TV with her boyfriend and his family at their home.

On Sunday, January 8, 1978, when Ted was arriving at the bus station in Tallahassee, Janet was still fast asleep in her warm bed after a late night at a friend's birthday party.

During the week leading up to the Chi Omega massacre, while Ted Bundy was securing a place at a rooming house known as The Oak, unsuccessfully seeking employment, stealing credit cards and other personal property of others, and stalking the unsuspecting prey of his new hunting ground, Janet Lester was doing homework, hanging out with her friends, helping her mom, babysitting her brother, taking pictures, riding her horse, working at her stepdad's store, and being a truly kind and generous person.

During the early morning hours of January 15th, just a little less than a month before she would vanish off the face of the earth forever, Janet was sleeping the restful, peaceful sleep of the guileless as Ted Bundy was bludgeoning and biting and brutalizing. Earlier in the day, she and

Kathy had driven into Dothan and spent the day shopping. Among other things, Janet had found the dress she would wear in the Miss Valentine pageant and a silky, sexy negligee to surprise Ben with on their upcoming anniversary.

Truly happy, Janet had no reason to doubt that her ecstatic existence would go on for at least another fifty years or more. Like the young women sound asleep in their beds in their rooms at the Chi Omega house, there was nothing in her experience to suggest that evil like that inside of and unleashed by Ted Bundy existed anywhere but horror films—or that, even if it did, it could enter uninvited a life like hers.

As Margaret Bowman, Lisa Levy, Kathy Kleiner, and Karen Chandler lay sleeping in their beds, dreaming sorority girl dreams, they couldn't have dreamt of the transformation and deterioration of the handsome young man who used to lure his victims into his car by pretending to be injured and in need of help. Nor could that same nightmare have revealed that the killer of women in Colorado was close enough to call on them that very night.

The demon inside Bundy was devouring him. No longer confident, suave, sophisticated, his demeanor was that of a disheveled man on his way to presenting as fully deranged.

In Sherrod's, the nightclub close to Chi Omega and where many of the sorority sisters went on a regular basis, he leered lasciviously, all but licking his lips like a gross glutton at a buffet trough.

Bundy, who used to blend in, who had actually believed himself to be invisible, now stood out as odd, strange, not quite right.

Both Chi Omega murder victims were there. Had

Ted seen them? Is this where predator spotted prey? Or
had he already planned to visit Chi Omega later that night?
Sometime after midnight and before the attacks, a man in
the parking lot of Sherrod's asked a passing young woman,
"Are you a Chi O?" When she responded that she wasn't,
he said, "You're lucky."

At around three in the morning, Nita Neary, an attractive, young blond coed, returned to Chi Omega following a date with her boyfriend and found the door unlocked.

After kissing her boyfriend goodnight, she closed
and locked the door behind her, then began turning off
lights that had been left on in the lower level of the sorority house. As she did, she heard up above her the sound of
someone running down the hallway. Moments later, as she
was headed to the stairs, she abruptly stopped in the foyer as a man wearing a blue toboggan cap, blue jacket, and
light-colored pants rushed down the stairs and crouched
at the door. He was carrying what she later described as a
large stick—the thick piece of oak firewood still dripping
with blood he had used as a weapon of unbelievable brutality.

Unaware of the unimaginable slaughter awaiting
discovery just up the stairs, Nita locked the front door and
made her way up to the upper floor, waking her roommate,
Nancy Dowdy, and returning downstairs with her to double
check everything and ensure it was truly secure.

When the two young woman went back upstairs,
they woke up Jackie McGill, the house president, to let her
know what Neary had witnessed. As they did, Karen Chandler staggered out of her room holding her bleeding head,
dazed, in shock, moaning quietly, pleading for help and
understanding.

As Janet Leigh Lester still slept in her bed some sixty-six miles away, the sorority sisters of Chi Omega phoned the Tallahassee Police Department and Tallahassee Memorial Hospital, and then discovered Kathy Kleiner, Karen Chandler's roommate, sitting in her bed, rocking back and forth, bleeding, hurting, uncomprehending.

Inside Chandler and Kleiner's room, there was blood on the beds, blood on the walls, blood on the windows, blood on the light fixture, blood on the ceiling—blood and oak bark everywhere.

Slowly, the sorority house woke up from all the noise and activity, one by one the young women waking and wandering out of their rooms.

There was no way they could know or realize its significance at the time, but the most telling detail during this period was which girls didn't wake, didn't open their doors, didn't stumble out sleepily to see what all the commotion was about.

Margaret Bowman and Lisa Levy didn't open their doors. They weren't able to and never would again.

Bludgeoned, beaten, bitten, garroted, assaulted, sodomized, violated in unconscionable ways while sleeping in their beds—a sleep that would soon become the eternal sleep of death. But did that sleep of death end their heartache and the thousand natural shocks their flesh was heir to, and what dreams came when their mortal coils had been so savagely shuffled off for them?

As police and EMTs were dealing with the massacre at Chi Omega, Bundy was still out in the night, stalking prey beneath cover of darkness, the bloody oak log still in his hand.

At some time around four that morning in an apartment off Dunwoody Street, Debbie Ciccarelli heard her neighbor, Cheryl Thomas, crying and pleading, followed by a loud pounding sound. Then nothing—an eerie, frightening silence. Debbie and her roommate, Nancy, tried calling Cheryl's apartment to check on her.

They could hear the phone ringing through the thin wall between them and the sounds of someone walking around the apartment, but Cheryl didn't answer.

She couldn't.

She had been savagely assaulted with the oak log, her face and head pounded with brutal blunt-force trauma.

The footsteps were those of Theodore Bundy prepping to strangle and rape Cheryl Thomas—he already had her pajama bottoms and panties down and a pair of nylon stockings at the ready—but the movements of Debbie and Nancy next door and their incessant phone calls had interrupted him. Now unable to anally rape her while choking the life out of her, the acts that seemed to have given Bundy the most sick satisfaction, he quickly masturbated on the bed beside her and crawled back out of the window he had entered through just a short while before.

With a dislocated shoulder, a broken jaw, a skull fractured in five places, and permanent deafness and equilibrium issues that ended her dance career, Cheryl Thomas was traumatized but alive—thanks to her friends, escaping a far, far worse fate at the hands of the man who would later describe himself as "the most cold-hearted son of a bitch you'll ever meet."

But Bundy was far worse than that. Cold-hearted doesn't begin to describe the cruel evil he was capable of, the pitiless savagery and sexual sadism he practiced and perfected without regard or remorse.

When day broke on the morning after the massacre, Tallahassee and FSU in general and the lives of certain coeds in particular would never be the same, but as Janet Lester opened her eyes on that Sunday morning, her idyllic existence seemed exactly as it was when she had drifted off into peaceful sleep the night before. And maybe it was. But it wouldn't be for long. For the fateful clock of her allotted time was already running backward, counting down toward the D-day of her tragic destiny.

Chapter Nine

On Sunday morning, January 15th, Janet Lester wasn't the only one whose days were numbered. Ted Bundy, too, had a date with destiny. He was exactly one month away from finally being captured and kept in a cage for the remaining eleven years of his loathsome life.

Of course, he didn't know it at the time.

For him, life continued in much the same way it had since he had escaped from the jail cell in Colorado. It wasn't just stolen time he was living on, but stolen property and identities too. He continued pilfering cash, credit cards, identities, cars, and anything else his bent mind told him he was entitled to.

He continued living large, frequenting fancy restaurants, sports equipment stores, tobacco shops, buying, at other people's expense, any and everything that suited his unhinged whimsy.

Who did he kill during this time? How many attempted assaults did he commit?

I knew Dad believed there were other open unsolved homicides that were most likely the work of Bundy—and he had often mentioned trying to clear them too—but he was personally responsible for the Janet Lester case and felt a much greater responsibility over it. It would always come first. He couldn't even consider investigating any others before solving once and for all the one he was ultimately answerable for.

On February 8th, Bundy stole a white FSU van and drove one hundred fifty miles east on I-10 to Jacksonville. He approached fourteen-year-old Leslie Parmenter, the daughter of a Jacksonville detective, in a Kmart parking lot across from Jeb Stuart Junior High School. Flashing her an unconvincing badge and identifying himself as "Richard Burton, fire department," he attempted to converse with the young teen, who described him as unkempt and agitated as he awkwardly tried to engage her. Unlike his early suave and sophisticated approaches of young coeds, Bundy, wearing dark-framed glasses, plaid pants, and a blue navy pea coat, abruptly stopped his van in front of the teen, leaving the door open.

Immediately suspicious of the odd and awkward man, Parmenter was guarded and confused.

As Bundy continued his attempt at inane conversation, Leslie's brother, Danny, pulled up in his truck, stuck his head out the window, and asked Leslie what the man wanted. After instructing Leslie to get into his truck, Danny approached Bundy and asked him what he wanted. "N-Nothing . . ." Bundy stammered. "I just asked if she was somebody else and just asked who she was."

As Bundy jumped back into his van, rolled up the window, and drove away, Danny quickly jotted down his license plate number and attempted to follow the van, but soon lost him in the heavy traffic.

That night, Bundy checked into a Holiday Inn in Lake City. As he ate dinner at the hotel and had drinks in the bar, the staff and other guests described him as weird, either drunk or spaced out, and unkempt, his hair greasy, dark, and dirty.

Leaving the Holiday Inn the next morning, Bundy headed down US 90 for a couple of miles and saw Lake City Junior High School.

As if the day was crying for what was about to befall little Kimberly Diane Leach, rain drops fell out of a gray sky of clouds.

Moving slowly down Duval Street in the rain, Bundy spotted the twelve-year-old crossing the schoolyard between the main building and a detached portable. She was returning to her first-period classroom to retrieve her purse, which she had left there in her rush to get to her second-period class. Jerking the van around to the other side of the road and jumping out, Bundy rushed up to the startled and vulnerable young girl. Grabbing her by the arm, Bundy pulled the frightened young girl over to his van and thrust her inside.

The vicious inhuman and all-too-human killer transported the young girl nearly thirty miles to Live Oak, where he pulled the van into a secluded rural area to rape, kill, and dump the body of what had just a short while before been a happy child looking forward to going shopping for her Valentine's Day dance after school.

Returning to Tallahassee with his mask of sanity back in place, Ted went on a date with a young woman from his rooming house that night. After abducting, subduing, brutalizing, raping, stabbing, cutting, killing, and dumping the body of little Kimberly Diane Leach in an old pigpen earlier in the day, Bundy dined at Chez Pierre with Francis Messier, eating good food and drinking fine wine in the company of an attractive young woman—all on a stolen credit card, of course.

From out in the other room, I hear Dad cough and say something.

Jumping up, I go check on him.

Chapter Ten

The dim, quiet house is warm and stuffy.

In the living room I find both men snoring.

Lying flat out on the couch, his hand over his heart as if saying the pledge of allegiance, Jake appears not to have moved at all since I eased him down there.

Dad stirs and starts coughing again.

Stepping into the tiny kitchen, I run a glass of water from the tap, and return with it to find him snoring again.

In another moment he moans and says something incomprehensible in his sleep.

The next time he coughs, he stirs and opens his eyes. Seeing me standing there startles him and he jumps, bringing up his hands in a defensive posture.

As a child, I was always startled by the way he so often startled awake, and some of the old familiar feeling fluttered deep inside me now.

"Dad, it's me. You were coughing. Here's some water."

"Huh?"

His eyes are bloodshot, the brows above them in need of trimming and, like the graying brown hair on his head, standing up.

Narrowing his eyes and blinking a bit, he seems to be having difficulty focusing.

"What're you doing here?" he asks.

Like his cough, I wonder if his bloodshot eyes and trouble focusing have anything to do with him being sick and are really signs of a deeper, darker infirmity beneath—a thought that would not have occurred to me had Jake not said what he did.

"Brought Jake home from the bar," I say.

He nods knowingly. "Knew someone would have to when he left to go out there. Figured I'd get a call. Must have fallen asleep."

He still hasn't taken the water from my outstretched hand.

"Drink some water," I say. "How are you feeling?"

He takes the water and drinks some, a small rivulet of which runs down the red-hued skin of his white-whiskered chin.

Coughing again, he chokes a little, but only pauses a moment for it to pass before finishing off the glass.

Jake stirs for the first time, licks his lips, adjust his body on the couch a bit, but doesn't wake.

"How bad was he?" Dad asks.

I shake my head. "He was fine. Just a little lost at the moment."

He nods and holds the glass out for me. "Thanks."

I take it. "Can I get you anything else? Help you to bed?"

He shakes his head. "I'm good here."

"Let me know if you need anything. I'll be in the spare room looking through the Janet Lester case."

His eyes widen. "Really?"

"We've been back a while. That's what I've been doing."

He nods, a small suppressed smile twitching his lips a bit. "I missed something. Hope you find it. Want to close it once and for all this time."

"Jake said you were sick," I say.

He shakes his head. "Don't want to talk about it. Going back to sleep."

I nod and head back toward the kitchen with the empty glass.

With his eyes closed, he says, "Been having a few symptoms. Brown sent me for blood work."

Our GP, Raymond Brown, is the old country doctor in Pottersville.

"Results are on the table," he adds. "We can talk about it tomorrow. Night."

"Night."

"And John," he adds, still without opening his eyes, "thanks for looking at the book on Janet."

"Should have sooner," I say. "Sorry I didn't."

Placing the glass in the sink, I step over and sit down at the old, compact, rickety kitchen table. Propped against the wall, held in place by a wooden napkin holder, is a small stack of mail. Sifting through it, I find the one from Dr. Brown.

In it are photocopies of the lab results, a note from the doctor in a thin, shaky, barely legible cursive, and a couple of printouts of articles about additional tests and treatment options if they confirm what Dr. Brown already knows to be the case.

By reading and rereading the contents of the envelope and Googling the questions they raise, I think I am able to understand.

The blood work Dr. Brown ordered for Dad included a complete blood count or CBC, a broad blood test to screen for a wide range of conditions and diseases. The results showed a markedly elevated level of lymphocytes.

Brown wants to do further testing, including a bone marrow examination that could confirm that Dad has chronic lymphocytic leukemia, or CLL, a not uncommon condition for a man his age.

Chronic lymphocytic leukemia is a type of cancer that starts from cells that become lymphocytes, certain white blood cells found in the bone marrow. The cancer or leukemia cells start in the bone marrow but then go into the blood. In CLL, the leukemia cells often build up slowly over time, and many people don't have any symptoms for at least a few years.

Based on the language used in Dr. Brown's note, and knowing Dad the way I do, my guess is he is being resistant to additional testing.

Folding the pages back the way they were and returning them to the envelope, I replace the envelope where I found it and walk back out into the living room, wanting to hug my dad, to wake him and hear his voice.

He is sleeping soundly, as is Jake, and I find the little noises, breaths, and snores they're both making comforting.

Though it's August in Florida and the single window unit running in the back bedroom can't cool the entire house, and though it's warmer out here where they are sleeping than anywhere else but the kitchen, I retrieve two flat sheets from the narrow linen closet at the end of the hall and drape one over each of them before returning to the spare room and the murder book awaiting me there.

Chapter Eleven

Janet Lester was an active, involved, busy young woman. Between school, work, photography, her horse Cinnamon, family obligations, friends, and a boyfriend, she didn't have much spare time. But sometimes she just liked to take it easy, chillin' out in front of the tube with her little brother, sometimes her mom, and on rare occasions her stepdad.

Ralphie liked *The Bionic Man, Man from Atlantis,* and *CHIPS*, which she watched with him when she could, but she liked shorter, lighter shows like *Happy Days* and *Laverne and Shirley* or *One Day at a Time* and *The Jeffersons.* Her stepdad liked *Three's Company*, but she didn't care for it. Everybody, including her mom, liked *Charlie's Angels.*

This is how she was spending the little life she had left—riding her horse, snapping pictures, lying on the shag carpet in front of the TV—while Ted Bundy was preparing to leave Tallahassee.

News of the Chi Omega murders had spread across the country, and cops who had investigated and arrested Bundy in Colorado and other places began traveling to Florida, believing that the authorities here were dealing with the same coed killer. Tallahassee in particular and Florida in general were no longer safe places for Bundy to hide.

While Janet and the other girls of Marianna High

School were preparing for and participating in the Miss Valentine pageant, Ted Bundy was stealing tags and credit cards and cars in an attempt to flee Tallahassee.

After some failed attempts and a close call with a cop, Bundy finally managed to steal a car on the evening of February 12th—a '72 orange VW that belonged to Ricky Garzaniti, who had left his keys in his car while dashing into the babysitter's house to pick up his child and gotten detained a bit.

That same night, Janet and Ben attended the Sweethearts' Ball, and for the second time that weekend a crown had been placed on Janet's head. Crowned king and queen of the Sweet-hearts' Ball after Janet had been crowned Miss Valentine 1978 the night before, Ben and Janet were having one of the best weekends of their short lives—one that was about to change in the most dramatic and horrific ways imaginable.

As Janet went home and pretended to go to bed, only to sneak out a short time later, Bundy was driving his stolen orange VW west on I-10 toward Pensacola and eventually the Alabama state line—though three days later he'd be arrested before reaching it.

After she was sure that her family was settled in for the night, Janet crept out of the house and to her car, which she had parked farther away than she normally did so no one would hear when she cranked it.

Making her way out of her neighborhood, she took a left on Highway 90 and a right at Highway 71—the rural road leading out to the old farmhouse where the party was.

As Janet was doing all this, Ted Bundy, some fifty miles from Tallahassee now, was cruising down I-10 watching the gas needle of the stolen VW bounce toward E.

An acquaintance from school, Little Larry Daughtry, worked at the Gulf station close to where Highway 71 ran beneath I-10. Daughtry's dad, Big Larry Daughtry, owned a liquor store just across the state line, and Little Larry sold booze to his underage classmates.

On her way to the party, Janet stopped by the Gulf station and purchased a bottle of Dewar's from Little Larry because she wanted to be as relaxed as possible.

At around this same time, a strange and agitated man with dark unkempt hair wearing light pants and a dark blue coat pulled his orange VW into the Gulf station and had Little Larry fill 'er up, paying the uneasy young attendant with a credit card.

The credit card turned out to be stolen and later Little Larry would pick Ted Bundy out of a lineup as the man who paid him with it, but he never could say for sure that the future murder victim and the infamous murderer had been there at the same time.

My phone vibrates and I withdraw it from my pocket to see that Anna has texted.

Anna: Woke up startled. Got worried when you still weren't here. You okay?

Me: Sorry. About to head that way.

Anna: Wake me if I fall back asleep. Let me know you're here.

Me: Will do. Love you.

Anna: Find out anything else about your dad?

Me: Yeah. It's not good. I'll tell you about it in the morning. Haven't really had a chance to talk to him yet.

Anna: Stay if you need to.

Me: Thanks, but I'll be heading that way in about 5 mins. Should be home in less than 20.

Anna: Be careful. Wake me when you get here. Love you.

I return the phone to my pocket.

I'm no longer single and I need to remember that— remember to be more considerate—especially of things that take me away from the house at night. Anna is understanding and supportive and enormously generous, allowing me a lot of leeway in the work I do and the hours I keep, but I've got to be better about managing my time away from her and our family.

I have even more questions now than when I started, and don't want to stop, but should be in bed beside Anna.

But being in bed beside Anna doesn't mean I have to be asleep.

As a compromise I decide to take the murder book with me so I can read it in the small beam of my battery-powered reading light.

Withdrawing another piece of paper from Dad's blue composition book, I leave him a note, letting him know I've taken the book and asking if we can talk in the morning before I leave for vacation.

I then check on Jake and Dad again and quietly ease out into the night.

Chapter Twelve

I place the murder book on the bedside table next to my reading light and climb into bed beside Anna.

Rolling over close to her, I gently kiss her on the cheek and whisper, "I'm home, baby. Sorry I was gone so long."

"Will you hold me?" she says.

"Of course."

She turns on her side and slides toward me and we begin to spoon, my mouth at her ear, my arms wrapped around her.

Turning her head slightly up, she says, "I'm so glad you're home."

"Me too."

"I must've had a bad dream because I woke up so scared, so worried about you. Then when you weren't here, I just . . . panicked a bit."

"I'm sorry. I should've just brought the murder book back here to begin with. Was stupid not to. Just wasn't thinking."

"No, I'm being silly," she says. "I know it's irrational, but I just haven't been able to shake it. And then once my mind got going . . . I just knew you were going to decide to not go on our vacation. I know you really don't want to anyway, and I thought, now he's got his excuse. I hate feeling like this. I know I'm being neurotic and I hate that."

I pull her even closer to me, hold her even tighter.

"I'll be fine by first light," she says. "And if you want to stay with your dad or get to work on the case, I'll understand. Just had a little meltdown. I just got you and I don't want to lose you."

"I'm not going anywhere—except on vacation with you."

"Really?"

"Of course. We're going to have a wonderful time. You deserve a getaway. I just wish it was just us—or us and our girls."

"I know. Sorry Johanna can't be there—and that my folks will be, but . . ."

"We'll have a great time. Can't wait to walk along the Gulf at sunset holding your hand."

"Thank you, John."

Taylor's rhythmic breathing coming from the baby monitor changes, and I can feel Anna's body respond. Lifting her head slightly, tilting her ear toward the monitor, she listens.

Taylor stirs, makes a sucking sound, and then her breathing returns to how it was before.

After a few moments, Anna relaxes, the tension draining out of her body, and she lays her head back down.

"If it's okay, I'll bring the murder book and read through it after you guys go to bed."

"Of course."

"And I might have to come back for part of a day to take Dad to the doctor, but—"

"Of course," she says again. "How is he? What's he . . ."

I tell her.

"Oh John, I'm so sorry. Are you okay?"

I nod, my nose rubbing her cheek as I do. "I'd like to go talk to him before we leave in the morning."

"Of course," she says, then laughs a little. "I keep saying that."

"But of course," I say with a little laugh of my own. "Because you're so generous and accommodating. Best friend and wife ever. Now, get some sleep so I won't be the only well-rested one for our vacation."

That gets a real laugh from her. "You sleep less than anyone I know," she says.

"Doesn't mean I'm not well rested. Quality over quantity."

"Actually, that's exactly what it means. You need both and you don't get much of either. Don't think I haven't noticed that big blue binder on your nightstand. You're gonna return to it after I fall back asleep, aren't you?"

"The thought had crossed my mind."

But that's all it was—a thought. Nothing more. I may have even fallen asleep before Anna did, because I don't remember anything else until Dad's call came early the next morning.

Chapter Thirteen

"How far'd you get?" Dad asks.

"Not even through the background," I say. "It's very thorough. Well constructed."

"You act like you expect something else," he says.

I shake my head. "Not at all. Truth is . . . I had no expectations."

Having met at the Corner Café and ordered breakfast, we got it to go and crossed the street to eat at a picnic table in Lake Alice Park.

As usual, Dad is dressed in what for him has been a type of uniform. Like many old-timers in the area, and several sheriffs in the South and West, an aging and scuffed pair of cowboy boots peek out at the bottom of his simple pressed and pleated tan trousers, and an old straw cowboy hat with a chocolate leather band rests comfortably on the crown of his head. His shirt is a solid cotton button-down, the sleeves of which are never rolled up, even in August.

North Florida is filled with farms and cattle ranches and was home to the original crackers—cowboys who got their name from cracking their whips to herd cows—and boots and hats and cowboy culture lingers, though far more in Dad's generation than mine.

It's early and quiet. The sun has yet to crest the tree tops and burn off the dew. Everything is damp.

Alice is peaceful, placid, her still surface a mirror of the morning.

Though not the Sheol it will soon become, the day is already hot and humid, my shirt clinging to my already sweating body the way the dew-damp seat is to my pants.

"I was trying to think if I'd ever read one of your murder books before," I add.

"Probably not. Can't be many of them. Past forty years I've been a damn politician more than anything else," he says.

He picks around at his eggs and takes a bite of toast, but seems to have no appetite. As he does, I study him. He's lost some weight and has that lean, headed-toward-feeble look thin older men get.

Pale and frail, he appears weakened and unsteady, his hands shaking ever so slightly as he rakes the fork through his scrambled eggs and holds the slice of brownish buttered wheat toast.

"You did a great job with the book," I say. "I'm hooked. I want to know what happened to Janet, who's responsible for her disappearance, and where she is. But . . ."

"But?" he says, his eyebrows rising. "There's a *but?*"

"I came to talk about your blood work, what it means, what's next. We can get to the case later."

He shakes his head. "I came to talk about the case. We can get to that other stuff later."

"That *other stuff* is your health."

"And it's not gonna change much while we talk about this case."

Raised the way I was, by Jack Jordan, where I was, in the South, I was trained from an early age to respect and defer to elders, especially my dad, so of course that's what I do—but this time, not without a little bargaining.

"We can talk about the case first," I say. "But only if you promise to talk to me about the *other stuff* afterward."

He nods.

"I have your word?" I say.

"My word," he says, still nodding.

"Okay."

"I'm sure you have questions for me," he says, "but my first question for you is are you in? Are you gonna help me investigate it?"

I nod. "I am. I will. I will have to work it around several other things—including a family vacation that starts today, but yes. I'm in."

"I know you've got a lot on you," he says, "but this is important. The clock is ticking."

Always pushing. A chief character trait of Jack Jordan is that he pushes. It's often subtle, often gentle, but it's always there. He's always working on something and always pushing it, pushing at it, pushing you to help him with it. This is going to be no exception.

"The clock has been ticking for forty years," I say.

"Well, yeah, but it's about to run out. And I'm not just talking about my . . . the health stuff I'm dealing with. Do you know how many unsolveds in the Panhandle I think might be the work of Bundy?"

I shake my head.

"Five that are a very strong likelihood and another

four that are at least a possibility. So why am I working this case and not them?"

"This was your case."

He nods. "For a while it was. You're right. But I plan to eventually work all the cases—and hope to solve them before I'm through."

"So why this one first?" I say.

"It's not just that this one was my case, it's that it's my fault it didn't get cleared back when it should have. All the suffering of Janet's family, especially her mom—but of Ben's family too. All of it. It's my fault 'cause I didn't do my job, 'cause I didn't stick around to close it when I should have."

I nod.

"But that's not why the clock's ticking. And it doesn't have as much to do with my clock ticking as you think. It's because of the newly elected state's attorney. She has promised to bring charges in the case. Hell, it was actually part of her campaign platform. She has a mandate to clean house, end corruption and the good ol' boy network. She's accusing me of a cover-up, of letting Ben go because his dad was a friend of mine. She plans to file charges against him any day now."

"Are you sure he didn't do it? What made you clear him?"

"I don't think he did it, but I'm not as sure now as I was back then. If he did it, I want to be the one to find out and build the case against him. If he did it, he and his dad made a fool out of me."

"What made you clear him?"

"Why don't you read the rest of the book first and see what you think, and then we'll talk about it," he says.

71

I nod. "That's a good idea. Is it okay if I take it with me to Mexico Beach and read it as I can this week?"

"Yeah, but I was hoping you could finish it today and we could start working on it tomorrow."

"I've promised Anna not only to go on this vacation but to be fully present with her while I'm there."

"But—"

"That part is nonnegotiable," I say. "But, I should have plenty of time to finish the book soon. And I'll only be a half hour away. Maybe I can get away for an afternoon and we can drive to Jackson County and reinterview some witnesses."

He's obviously not satisfied by that, but he nods his resignation as he frowns and lets out a little sigh.

"Anything you want to ask me?" he says. "Anything stand out to you at this point? Or do you want to finish the book before we really delve into it?"

"Tell me about the blood in the car," I say. "What made y'all think it was Janet's?"

"It was AB negative—just like Janet's. It was female. Which is about all they could tell us back then. Why?"

"My first question of a supposed murder where there is no body. . ." I say. "Is she really dead? Was it her blood? Did she fake her own death in order to disappear?"

He nods. "I considered that but maybe not enough. There was nothing in her life and background—at least that I found—that made me think she would want to disappear. I mean nothing."

I think about it. We should dig deeper there to make sure that was actually the case.

"But the real reason I believed then that she was dead and still believe now that she is . . ."

72

"Yeah?"

"AB negative is a very, very rare blood type—the rarest—and no one could lose as much blood as was in that car and survive. The ME said so."

Chapter Fourteen

For my entire life, my dad has been as stable and consistent as anyone I've known. He has his quirks and he's held me at arm's length, but he's been constant—an unmoving anchor in our family, a fixed star in the night sky by which I have navigated my life.

For that to now be changing, shifting beneath my very feet, has me off balance, searching for stability and footing, finding none.

"What made you go to the doctor in the first place?" I ask.

We are similar in our avoidance of doctors, hospitals, and medication.

"Clothes kept growing," he says. "They were fallin' off me and I couldn't figure out why. Was tired all the damn time. Weird swelling in different part of my body—neck, underarms, stomach, and I was keeping a fever. It wouldn't go away. All that for long enough'll send anybody to the doctor. Even me."

I smile. "Just not as hardheaded as you used to be."

"That's a risk factor," he says.

"What is?"

"Old age. I'm less stubborn 'cause I'm less everything these days. Two main factors for CLL is oldness and whiteness. Tick those two boxes for damn sure."

"Did you read the information Brown sent with your blood work?" I ask.

He shrugs.

"You don't know for sure you even have it."

He smirks and gives me a *get real* expression. "Pretty sure."

"He wants to do a bone marrow test to make sure."

"Yeah," he says, "I don't know about that."

"What's not to know?"

"May just let it run its course. If it's my time, it's my time."

"The literature he sent said depending on a few factors, it can be treatable."

"Just not sure I want to spend my final days in a sterile room having poison pumped into my body."

"That's not how it would be. Plus it could give you many more days."

"*Could.*"

"Yes, could. Could give you more time to work this and other cases. Could give you far more time with your granddaughters."

He nods noncommittally. "I'm just so damn tired as it is."

"But that's most likely the leukemia. That will get better once we deal with it."

"Maybe," he says, his mouth twisting into a half frown. "I don't know. I think I'd just rather get my house in order, finish up what I can—including Janet's case."

"At least have the test and follow-up appointment with Brown so you can make an informed decision. Seems the least you can do for me if I'm going to solve your case for you."

His face breaks out into a big smile that makes him look twenty years younger and much less pale and frail.

"I'll do you one better," he says. "You solve this damn case, and I'll do the damn treatment."

Chapter Fifteen

I arrive home expecting to find Anna packed and ready to ride, but instead find her cleaning.

"I figured you'd be in the car waiting," I say.

Taylor is in her highchair at the kitchen table eating Cheerios with her small fingers, Anna scrubbing the grout of the tile floor near her.

She looks up at me with tears in her eyes.

I immediately kneel down beside her.

"What is it? What's wrong?"

"Mom fell and broke her wrist while she was packing up the car," she says.

"Oh no. How is she? Where is she? Does she have to have surgery? Are you okay?"

"I'm fine," she says. "I'm being silly again. She's going to be okay. They're not sure yet whether they're going to have to operate."

"I'm sorry, honey," I say. "What do we need to do? Go up there? Do they still plan to go to the beach?"

She shakes her head. "That's what I'm most upset about. The damn vacation. I was so looking forward to it. I . . . I just . . ."

"Need it," I say.

"Obviously," she says. "Look at me. I'm tearily cleaning the freakin' grout."

I smile.

"At least it's good news for you," she says. "Not only do you not have to leave your dad or the case, but you don't have to spend a week in a beach house with my parents."

"Listen to me," I say. "I know how much you've been looking forward to this, how much you need it, deserve it. There's no way we're not going. Unless your mom needs you up there, we're still going."

"Really?" she says, a small smile dancing at the corners of her lips.

"Really."

"I figured you'd use this as a chance to get out of going, that you'd be so relieved not to have to go that you'd—"

"Of course not. I wouldn't do that."

"So we can go?"

"Unless you'd rather stay and clean the grout."

She pretends to consider it, acting as if she's torn.

"Do you think we need to go to your folks? If we do, we can—and we'll turn even that into a vacation all its own. One way or another, you're getting away and relaxing."

"I'll double check, but she said she's okay, that there's nothing we can do. They told us to go ahead and use the cottage, but I didn't think you'd want to."

"Do you?" I ask.

"You know I do."

"Then you should know I do too."

Dropping the small brush she is scrubbing with, she

lunges toward me, arms outstretched for an embrace, wrapping me up in a big hug, but I'm unable to keep my balance from my kneeling position and her momentum carries us back. We fall to the floor, her on top of me.

"Are you okay?" she asks.

I nod. "But I think my skull may have put a chip in the tile."

Chapter Sixteen

The late afternoon sun splashes bright orange on the cumulus clouds above it while all around it the deep plum-colored sky slowly devolves into darkness.

Stillness. Peace. Breathtaking beauty.

I'm alone on an empty stretch of beach.

A weekday toward the end of August, school in, tourists from Alabama and Georgia returned home, nearly all of Mexico Beach is open and uninhabited these days.

Sitting on sand so white, so soft, so fine it has the consistency of refined sugar without the stickiness, I am mindful of my breathing and my thoughts.

Before me the green waters of the Gulf roll in and back out again, their crash and splash joining the airy sound of the wind to create an aural tunnel of forceful white noise, pierced intermittently by the screech and squeal of seagulls.

Closing my eyes momentarily on the elegance and magnificence, I breathe even more slowly. In and out. In and out. Conscious of my breathing. Mindful of my thoughts.

I've come to this secluded section of Mexico Beach to meditate and pray, to recalibrate and reconnect—activities that too often get crowded out by less important endeavors during my days.

Though I was less than enthusiastic about this retreat from the routine of our daily lives, I need this every bit as much as Anna, and I am grateful to be here.

Like a child fighting falling asleep—something else I too often do—my life would be far better if I would relax into opportunities like this one instead of fighting against some of the very things that are so good for me.

Over the course of my life, my spiritual practice has evolved and expanded, shifted and changed, but it has always included this—prayer and meditation in the splendor of North Florida nature.

Thoughts come and I let them go, observing but not engaging with them.

I breathe in the beauty.

I express my gratitude and my love.

Everything about my experience is restorative and nurturing, and I realize, as I always do, just how much richer and sweeter and deeper my life would be if I would just insist that this be a more consistent part of my daily routine.

Later toward evening, Anna and I walk hand in hand along the water's edge, and it is as much an act of worship and spiritual practice as my time alone on the beach had been.

"Can't tell you what it means to me that you insisted we still come," Anna says.

Taylor is asleep in the baby sling wrapped around her

body, her small head nestled against Anna's breasts.

It's after sundown and the quiet quality of evening bathes everything with an ethereal light and sound, like a palpable presence of transcendence flowing in and through and out of us.

"I was an idiot to be hesitant in the first place," I say.

We had already talked at length about my dad and her mom and even the Janet Lester case earlier in the day. Now it was time for all of that—along with everything else—to remain at bay and let it be, for a short while at least, as if we are the only two people on the planet.

"Sorry I've been on edge lately. It's like some of the shit we went through is finally catching up with me."

"You're handling everything extremely well," I say. "Don't hesitate to share it with me and let me help, and if you feel like you need to see a counselor, we'll find you the very best."

"I'm married to the very best."

We pause long enough for me to kiss her, then continue walking.

"You've been through so much," I say.

"Speaking of being married to the best," she says. "I know we are married in every way that truly matters, but . . . I'd like to do it officially."

"I guess I always figured we would as soon as your divorce from Chris comes through," I say.

"It arrived in the mail this morning."

I stop and drop to a knee without letting go of her hand.

"Anna, I have loved you since the moment I first met you when we were just children. I have always loved you. I will always love you. Of all the women in all the world, you are *the* woman to me. The only woman. You are my dream girl, my best friend, my partner in everything. You are my everything. I never again, not for one moment, want to experience life without you by my side. Will you marry me—"

"I will."

"I wasn't finished."

"Oh, please finish."

"—as soon as possible," I say.

She smiles as tears trickle down her cheeks.

"Yes," she says. "Yes. I thought you'd never ask."

She kneels down with me and we embrace and kiss, careful not to wake Taylor as we do.

Chapter Seventeen

Janet Lester had decided it was *time*, determined she was ready, while dancing with Ben to "How Deep Is Your Love" by the Bee Gees at the Sweethearts' Ball.

She had made him wait long enough, hadn't she?

Ben was a good guy, and he really cared for her, but he wasn't going to wait forever. He'd been sweet and patient, but she could tell he was really beginning to get frustrated. Them *not* doing it was becoming a big deal.

And what about her? Hadn't she waited long enough? She was eighteen. It was time for her too. She was the last of her friends to still be a virgin.

"I've got a surprise for you," she whispered in his ear as they slow danced beneath the disco ball, a million tiny spots of light slowly swirling around them.

She was wearing a beige dress with lots of ruffles similar to one she had seen Farrah Fawcett wear at a recent Hollywood premiere. He was wearing a brown suit with a beige shirt that matched her dress. They were surrounded by several other slow-dancing couples, but none that had been together a fraction of the time they had.

"Oh yeah?" he said. "What's that?"

He seemed distracted and maybe even a little disinterested—two things he seemed more and more these days.

Maybe it was because he was already drinking, but that wouldn't explain why he had been acting that way in general lately. More and more all the time.

Her waiting too long would explain it though. Had he lost interest in her?

"You okay?" she asked.

"Yeah. Why?"

"I don't know . . . you just seem a little . . . distracted."

He shrugged and shook his head, but didn't say anything to allay her concerns.

Was the song, the song that was playing when she decided to give herself to him, actually a warning? Should she have been questioning how deep his love was?

"What is it?" she asked. "What's wrong?"

"Nothin'. Why?"

"You just seem . . . I don't know. Like maybe you're . . ."

"I'm what? Let's just enjoy the song. I really dig it. You know? You're just trippin' tonight for some reason. You tired from last night? Or has bein' the queen gone to your head already? Just chill."

They danced in silence some more, her waiting to see if he'd mention the surprise.

He didn't.

Because he didn't care or because he was really enjoying their dance?

She was thinking of giving him her virginity, she'd bought a special negligee for the occasion and everything, and he totally didn't care.

Maybe rather than this being the night she gave herself to him, maybe this was the night they'd call it quits.

He was a stone fox and sweet to her most of the time, but . . . maybe he just didn't love her like he used to. Maybe he had his eye on someone else. But who? One name came to mind immediately. Sabrina. She flirted with him all the time. And everybody knew she was a sure thing. Sabrina Henry. It had to be.

Are they sleepin' together already? Is he distracted because he's looking for her while he's dancing with me? That's why he's been so understanding about waiting—because he hasn't been.

Stop dancing and walk off the floor right now. Leave him here to—

But before she could, the song came to an end and he lifted her chin and kissed her tenderly.

"I love you so much, Janet Leigh," he said. "Don't forget you were my queen before you were theirs. I don't know what I'd do without you in my life. Now, what's this surprise you've got for me? Is it a good surprise, or a real good surprise?"

Chapter Eighteen

I quietly flip through the witness statements, skimming each one in the faint splash of illumination provided by my reading light clipped to the murder book.

Beside me Anna is asleep. Her breathing and that of Taylor's coming through the small speaker of the baby monitor are the only sounds beside the occasional creak in the too-quiet cottage.

Earlier in the evening, we had walked down and eaten pizza at 40th Street Pizzaria and Seafood. The pizza was some of the best we'd had in a while, and we brought a second one back with us to warm up for a snack—something we didn't do, because Anna fell asleep before we could.

Our moonlit walk along the beach on the way back was romantic and buoying, and I figured we might go back out later for a swim or a longer walk, but when I came in from talking to Johanna on the phone a short while later, I found Taylor and Anna fast asleep.

I always miss Johanna, but it's particularly acute tonight. Something about us being here without her just doesn't seem right, and despite only being half an hour farther away from her, being out of my ordinary environment makes me feel less available for her somehow—even though on a rational level I know it's not the case.

I console myself with the fact that we'll be together again at the end of the week, but the constant dull and at times acute ache of missing her feels as though it's slowly hollowing me out inside.

The witness statements are pretty much what I'd expected they'd be, though perhaps a little more directly contradictory than usual.

Most of the young people at the party said they never saw Janet there, but a few did.

A classmate of hers, Charles Fountain, the only black student at the farmhouse that night, swore she was there and that he saw her not once but a handful of times throughout the night. He even described in detail what she was wearing—a cream crinkle-textured blouse with a lace yoke and a camel, tan, and rust floral-print skirt with a deep flounce at the bottom.

Dad had written, *How does a boy know so much about a girl's clothes?*

Answering his own question later, Dad discovered that Fountain planned to move to New York after graduation to study fashion design, and deduced that, although he couldn't be positive, the thin, soft-spoken black boy was most likely homosexual.

Fountain's only interest in Janet seemed to be as a friend—one mostly fascinated by her sense of fashion and her eye for photography.

Another witness, a young woman named Valerie Weston, who was actually closer to Janet—though not in each other's inner circles, they were part of the yearbook staff together—said Janet was definitely not there that night, that she spent a lot of time looking for her because she wanted to congratulate her for winning the Miss Valentine pageant and show her a totally awesome photograph she had taken. She said she definitely totally was a no-show that night. And only totally stunned spazzes would say that she was.

Ann Patterson, a junior who shared one class with Janet, remembered seeing her briefly and described her as wearing an outfit similar to the one Charles recalled—though not nearly in as much detail.

Kathy Moore, either Janet's best friend or biggest competitor depending on who was asked, said Janet did grace the party with her presence but only briefly, and that she never actually came inside the house.

This fits with what Gary Blaylock said. He said that while he was upstairs peeing, he looked out the window and not only did he see Janet but he saw Ben with her and the two of them drive off together in Janet's car.

In his statement, Ben said she never came—that she was supposed to, that he waited and waited for her, but that she never showed. Said he figured she couldn't sneak out, or fell asleep waiting for her family to go to bed. It had been a big, long weekend and she was exhausted. He was disappointed but he understood. Said he never saw her again after he took her home from the Sweethearts' Ball and didn't know anything was wrong until his mom woke him up the next morning saying that her stepdad was on the phone looking for her.

Though Ben never offered an alibi, he had one and it was offered for him. A girl named Sabrina Henry, who had always had a crush on Ben and who had always flirted with him and made sure he knew she was his for the taking, said he was with her, that they left the party together and were with each other the rest of the night.

The final witness from the farmhouse party wasn't at the party at all. A loner with a violent juvenile record who graduated the year before named Clyde Wolf said he was watching the comings and goings of the party from the woods in back of the pasture. He never stepped forward or volunteered any information, but once it was discovered he had been there, he was brought in and questioned by the investigators. He too said Janet was there that night, but never went inside, and that Ben climbed into her car and left with her.

Chapter Nineteen

"**W**hy didn't you arrest Ben Tillman for Janet's murder?" I ask.

"You finish the book?" Dad says.

"Finished the part where several witnesses have him leaving the party with Janet in her car—the same car she was killed in a short while later."

We are in his new, immaculate, white extended-cab GMC truck, but unlike any other time we ever have been, I am driving.

It's Tuesday afternoon and we are driving to Marianna to try to talk to Ben Tillman. We are coming from Dad's bone marrow test at his doctor's office in Panama City—something Anna set up and insisted he do sooner rather than later, something he agreed to when I told him we'd work the case for the remainder of the day once the test was done.

Dad is turned in the seat, leaning on his side, keeping pressure off the hip that was used for the aspiration and biopsy. So far it's sore but not extremely so, and though the wound is seeping, it has yet to soak the bandage or the loose jeans he's wearing.

"Maybe I should have," Dad says. "Came close to it

more than once during the investigation."

"So why didn't you?"

"It's kinda complicated," he says. "There wasn't just one reason. Bottom line is I didn't stay with the case as long as I should have. I should've seen it through, but . . . you kids were young, your mom and I were havin' a pretty rough time of it, I had my own department to run."

He doesn't say anything else but I sense there is more—other reasons why he stopped working the case when he did.

"I worked it as long as I could and then turned everything over to the state's attorney's office. He convened a grand jury. I think it was a tough decision for them, but the decision not to indict was theirs."

"Did you turn over the case to the state's attorney before you were finished investigating it thoroughly?"

I'm pressing him and I expect him to become defensive, but instead he just nods.

"I'm pretty sure I did," he says. "I didn't think so at the time—or I didn't want to think so, but even then part of me knew I was."

"So take me through why you did. I'm not understanding."

"I told you why."

"There's got to be more to it than that."

He shakes his head and I can tell that's all I'm going to get. I file it away to revisit later.

"The thing is, by the end of the investigation I didn't think he did it," Dad says. "I'm just wondering now if I was wrong."

"So what said he didn't do it?" I say.

"The girl, Sabrina Henry, swore under oath he was

with her. She never wavered and we were never able to break her. There was no physical evidence against him—beyond a few fingerprints in her car that could be explained by him being in it at an earlier time. As her boyfriend he would've been. Would've been far more suspicious if there hadn't been any. His mom said she got up to go to the bathroom in the middle of the night and looked in on him, and he was in his bed sleeping soundly. We knew what he wore from pictures taken at the party. We tested his clothes, which were still on the floor of his bedroom, and didn't find any blood or other evidence on them—and they hadn't been washed. Still had beer that he spilled at the party on them. And I thought then and I still think now there's a very good chance Ted Bundy did it."

Marianna is an interesting place. A small town of less than seven thousand people, it's a naturally beautiful place—like so many in North Florida—with a diverse landscape of massive old oak trees, their spreading branches draped with Spanish moss, tall North Florida pines, the Chipola River, Blue Hole Spring, and the Mariana caverns, a series of dry, air-filled caves with stunning formations of limestone stalactites, stalagmites, soda straws, flowstones and draperies.

Unlike my flatter part of Florida, Marianna is hilly, the large farms surrounding it consisting of sloping croplands and pastures of rolling hills.

Founded in 1828 by a Scottish entrepreneur named Scott Beverege who named the town after his wife Mary and her friend Anna, it became the county seat the following year.

Platted along the Chipola River just below the Alabama state line, Marianna and the broader Jackson County is known for extremely fertile soil, which is why so many plantation owners from other states like North Carolina relocated here back then.

And it's not just the soil, Marianna is rich with history too. It's where the Confederate governor of Florida, John Milton, is buried. It's the scene of a Civil War battle between a small home guard of boys, old men, and wounded soldiers and a contingent of some seven hundred Federal troops. It is also the site of the savage torture and brutal lynching of Claude Neal, an African American man accused of rape and murder in 1934. Marianna is also the home to Dozier School for Boys, an infamous reform school operated by the state of Florida, which for a time was the largest juvenile reform institution in the United States. Throughout its over one-hundred-year history, the school was a place of brutality, of abuse, beatings, rapes, torture, and murder. Marianna is, of course, also the place of the Broken Heart Miss Valentine Murder of Janet Leigh Lester, which to this day remains unsolved.

Looking at Marianna's quaint main street of restored old buildings, its historic district of ancient churches and antebellum homes, and its breathtaking natural beauty, it's hard to fathom so many horrific things have happened here.

Chapter Twenty

Ben Tillman was Marianna High School's star baseball player, taking his team to state during his junior year, coming just two runs short of bringing home the championship.

It was believed he'd do the same in his senior year, only more successfully, but then his girlfriend was murdered, he was suspected, and his life unraveled.

Before the Broken Heart Murder case, Ben was popular and respected.

Ben was cute in a boyish way, but it was his genuine niceness that caused most of the girls at Marianna High to find him so attractive. That said, he was strikingly photogenic and model good-looking in the many photographs Janet took of him over their years together. Nearly all in black and white, Janet's photographs of Ben were dramatic and artistic and revealed a depth and complexity Ben rarely revealed to anyone else.

The son of the sheriff of Jackson County, Ben was neither a bully, a punk, nor a rat. Although always careful not to break the law, except for a little underage drinking, he never made the other kids feel guilty or like they were being watched for the illicit or illegal activities they engaged in.

Loyal to his friends, faithful to his longtime girlfriend, Ben was liked by his fellow students and well regarded by his teachers and the school administrators.

Apart from a few rumors about him having a pretty nasty temper, which was rarely if ever witnessed and not given much credence by most, Ben was believed to be about as perfect as an adolescent young man could be.

There is little left of any of that in the middle-aged man whose face shows the signs of a hard life or hard living, or both, standing before me now.

I can't find even a trace of the effervescent and athletic young baseball player who was smart and attractive enough to steal Janet's heart in the too-thin, brittle-boned, sun-damaged, unkempt husk of a man hunched from carrying the invisible weight of this across all these years.

Unable to ever really get over what happened, Ben hadn't accepted the baseball scholarships he had been offered. He had never left Marianna, never attended college, never married, never had kids, never had a decent job.

Never had a job at all. Not really. No one in town would hire him.

He has spent decades mowing grass. He doesn't even do it under a business name, just as a cash-only odd-job approach like a grammar school kid using his parents' mower over the summer.

We find him at the old Marianna High School building loading his mower into a rickety and rusting old trailer hitched to his rickety and rusting old Ford Ranger.

He had started shaking his head the moment I got out of the truck and walked toward him.

"Told you I wouldn't talk to him," he says.

When I called earlier and told him what we were doing and asked if he'd talk to us, he had said he would never speak to Dad again, which is why I asked Dad to stay in the truck while I tried to speak to Ben.

"Will you talk to me?" I ask. "If he stays in the truck. Will you just talk to me for a few minutes?"

He shakes his head, but there's no real conviction in it. He then looks from me over toward the truck. "He ruined my life."

His life was ruined the night of February 12th—whether he killed Janet or not—and from what I could tell, Dad hadn't done anything to make it worse, but I don't say anything.

"Sure, he didn't kill Janet and he didn't arrest me, but he didn't clear me, didn't catch who really did it. Cost my dad the next election and left everyone around here to suspect me for the rest of my life." He lets out a harsh laugh. "Haven't had a life. Not really."

This decimated man, this later iteration of Ben Tillman, has the skinny, bleak, raw-boned, bloodshot look of an alcoholic, and though it's early afternoon and he's at work, I can smell the cheap liquor on his breath.

"You think he did it intentionally?" I ask. "Or just failed to solve the case?"

"Comes to the same damn thing, don't it? Either way. It's the same."

Violent crime, particularly murder, breaks people, makes hollowed-out shells of previously vibrant people. And it does so to the criminals and cops no less than the loved ones left behind in the vacuous absence of the victim.

I nod toward the brown brick buildings behind him. "This is where y'all went to school, isn't it?"

He turns and looks at it and nods slowly.

We are quiet for a few moments.

The midday sun looms high above us, radiating stifling bands of heat that seem concentrated directly on us. He had been sweating when I arrived. Now we both are. Hair and clothes damp, skin moist and clammy, beads of perspiration trickling down backs and faces.

"Lot of people's lives peaked here," he says. "But mine didn't."

I wait but he doesn't say anything else. "No?"

"My life didn't peak in high school. It ended."

I nod. The truth of what he's saying is etched in the lines of his face, written in the sad song behind his eyes.

It's disconcerting to even think of this broken older man as the boy I've been picturing, the one dancing with Janet at the Sweethearts' Ball, the one she decided to give herself to as they danced to "How Deep Is Your Love," the one Sabrina Henry and so many other young women had such a crush on.

"Can we talk about that night?" I ask, not having to identify it in any other way.

For him and those like him, there is only one *that night*. For the truly fortunate, most of whom have no idea just how fortunate they are, there is no single night that is *that night*, that is *the* night by which life is divided into before and after.

He shakes his head. "Nothing to say. Said it all then, and a goddamn lot of good it did me. Got nothing to add. Janet didn't show up that night. Period. I didn't see her. I didn't kill her. I didn't have anything to do with it. I don't know who did."

"What about those who swore under oath they saw her there?" I say.

"Only two possibilities. They're lying or mistaken."

I don't point out that another possibility is that he is.

The August heat draws the sour smell of booze and cigarette smoke and body odor out of his pores as if vapors from precipitation after a recent rain, and he smells like an old diesel engine converted to now run on rotting food byproducts.

"More than one person said they saw you leave with her," I say.

"See previous answer. They couldn't have seen me do something I not only didn't do, I couldn't do—*because she wasn't there*. She stood me up. Broke my heart at first. Then I figured she was just tired and fell asleep. Later I realized while I thought she was blowing me off or sleeping through what was supposed to be the best night of our lives because being crowned queen two nights in a row took too much out of her, she was actually being murdered."

"What about Sabrina Henry saying you were with her?"

"See previous answer. Only two possibilities."

"I can't see how she could be mistaken about something like that," I say.

"So," he says, "only one possibility. She's lying. Why? I couldn't tell you. What I can tell you is that someone viciously and savagely murdered the only girl I've ever loved. And he took her, so we couldn't even bury her. I don't know how. I don't know why. I don't know who. What I do know is Janet's life wasn't the only one he took that night."

Chapter Twenty-one

Sabrina Henry, now Gibbs, has the manic, uptight, slightly crazed-eyes look of someone desperately trying to hold everything together.

In high school she had been mostly on the fringes because the guys didn't respect her and the other girls didn't trust her. Back then she was seen as sort of slow and shallow and mostly annoying. She had a good, well-developed body and a prettyish face, but she wasn't likable. Most of the guys who slept with her only did so once, privately confiding in each other that as good as her body was and as easy and effortless as it was to take her off into the woods or somebody's empty river camp, it wasn't worth the aggravation of listening to her on the way there and back.

Now a middle-aged woman with extra weight and a fading allure, she resembles Patsy Ramsey, the former beauty queen mother of the murdered six-year-old JonBenét, killed in her own home in Boulder, Colorado, on Christmas night in 1996. She has the same dyed-black hair, big blue-green eyes, immaculate makeup, and bright red lipsticked lips.

We meet with her on the pool patio behind her huge

home beneath the shade of a large umbrella rising out of a wrought iron table.

A pitcher of lemonade and glasses with ice in them along with some sort of simple short-bread cookie are on a tray on the table waiting for us when we arrive.

Without apology or explanation, she tells us to park on the street down a little ways and walk around the side of the house to the gate of the tall wooden privacy fence.

"I remember you always being respectful and kind to me," she says to Dad. "Didn't get a lot of that back then. I really appreciated that."

Dad nods and tips the old cowboy hat he's wearing, then shakes her outstretched hand. "Was my pleasure, ma'am. This is my son, John. We sure do appreciate you taking the time to talk to us."

I shake her hand and we all take a seat around the table.

"Speaking of time," she says, "I'm sorry, but I don't have much at all."

"We understand," Dad says.

He's got his full Southern-gentleman charm flowing, which seems to me manipulative, insincere, and even condescending, but she seems not to see it that way at all.

"The truth is," she says, as she pours lemonade into glasses and passes them to us, "I wouldn't have agreed to meet anyone else. Like I said, you were very good to me back then. Even still, what happened to Janet that night has destroyed a lot of lives. I determined a long time ago it wasn't going to destroy mine. So I've left the past in the past. But . . . I so want justice for Janet. It . . . does my heart . . . I just appreciate that you haven't given up on finding out what happened to her. But I really, really want to keep this little chat just between us. None of the people in my life now have any idea about any of this—or that I was even . . . involved."

"Including your husband?" Dad asks.

"Especially him."

Her husband, a wealthy cattleman fifteen years her senior, owns and operates a cattle farm and processing plant of several thousand acres and worth several million dollars between Mariana and Dothan, and is rumored to be a severe, humorless man as stern with his wife as he is his business.

"Can you tell us what you think happened to her?" I ask.

Without her seeing, Dad shoots me a look that lets me know he'd rather handle the questions.

"Some absolute madman savagely murdered her and hid her body somewhere where no one could find it. It's the only explanation. No one I know—or knew back them—could have done that. No one. It had to be a monster passing through."

"Like Ted Bundy," I say.

"Yeah, maybe, I guess. I heard he was around here that night. Is that true?"

Dad gives me the look again.

"He was," Dad says. "But we really just want to hear what you remember from that night."

Her gaze drifts up and away from us. "I just remember everybody bein' happy. Carefree. For the last time. I guess we had the normal high school drama that we thought mattered so much, but it really was so nothing. You know? It was the last time we were ever just innocent kids. After that we always had this dark cloud hanging over us."

"Have you remembered anything over the years since we last spoke that you didn't remember back then?" Dad says.

She starts to answer, but stops as he adjusts in his seat and winces in pain.

"Are you all right?" she asks.

He nods. "Just got a sore hip. That's all. What were you about to say?"

"I'm sure it's nothing and you probably read all kinds of things wrong after something like that happens, but . . . I just remember Kathy Holmes arriving late that night and being all out of sorts. She was never late for anything. Ever. It's the only time I can remember her being late. And I'd never seen her act like that before. She was always with it, but that night she was a basket case."

"Who?" Dad asks. "I don't recall anybody by that—"

"Sorry. It's her married name now. Kathy Moore. Janet's best friend. I'm sure she had nothing to do with it—a girl couldn't really do something like that, could she? But it's just what came to mind when you asked if I had thought of anything else over the years."

"What was her relationship with Janet like?" Dad says.

"A little strange, to be honest. Like love-hate. She seemed like she really liked Janet sometimes, then others she acted so . . . I don't know . . . like jealous, but more. Like she wanted to be her . . . or . . . replace her. I'm probably reading way too much into this now. So please take it with a . . . just for what it's worth. But it's my honest opinion of how it was. She works up at Sunland but she should probably be a resident."

Sunland Center is a community serving some five

hundred individuals with intellectual and developmental disabilities housed in an old air force base up on Highway 71 between Marianna and Greenwood.

"You ever talk to Ben Tillman?" I ask.

"Ben? No. Why?"

Getting no look from Dad this time, I proceed.

"Y'all aren't close?"

"Never were. I sure feel bad for the guy. I just can't imagine what he's . . . But no, we haven't spoken a single word since that night."

"So you have no reason to lie for him."

"Right. I liked Ben. Had a crush on him. But I wouldn't lie for anyone—especially if they could've killed someone else."

"And he was with you that night?"

"He was. I swear it on my life. I have no reason to lie. If anything, I have reason to lie against him—if I was that sort of person. Like I said, he never spoke to me again. I tried so many times."

"Why do you think he didn't use you as an alibi?" I ask.

She shakes her head. "I have no idea. Guilt, I guess. I really don't know. My guess is if it had come down to him actually going to jail he might have, but . . . as it was . . ."

"Y'all were together at the party and—"

She jumps up suddenly. "That's the garage door opening," she says.

I can hear a slow mechanical sound and various creaks and clicks coming from the other side of the wall to our right.

"It's my husband. You've got to go. Now."

She seems genuinely panicked, the crazed look in her eyes intensifying.

"Please. Come on."

She grabs our glasses, pours the remainder of their contents back into the pitcher, then tosses them into the pool.

"Please hurry. He knows nothing about any of this. He only moved to town about ten years ago."

We stand and begin to make our way across the patio, Dad limping, moving slowly.

She quickly walks to the wooden gate, opens it, and ushers us through it when we finally make it there.

"I've finally got a good life," she says. "I can't jeopardize it for a case that's probably never gonna be solved anyway."

Chapter Twenty-two

"**H**ow do you have people who knew her equally well disagreeing on whether she was there or not that night?" Anna says.

"Eyewitnesses," Merrill says. "Only thing worse than one is more than one."

I smile.

I'm truly happy to have Merrill Monroe, my closest friend since childhood, here with us. As a surprise for me, Anna had invited him to the beach house for dinner and he was here waiting on me when I returned from my day in Panama City and Marianna with Dad.

We are now sitting at a table on the deck at Toucan's, a large, wooden ocean-side restaurant, the last of the setting sun only an orange glow sinking into the green Gulf.

Taylor is in a highchair at the end of the wooden booth, being spoon fed veggies by Anna and slipped Cheerios by Merrill.

This is the last night of our vacation, which I found out this evening is being cut short because Anna's mom needs her help after all. Tomorrow Anna and Taylor will travel to Dothan to help care for her mom. I will use the time off I already have to help Dad reinvestigate Janet Lester's disappearance, traveling to Anna's parents' farm in Dothan to stay each evening when Dad and I are done.

"I know eyewitnesses are notoriously unreliable," Anna says, "but this isn't that exactly, is it? It's not like there was an accident or event and they saw different things. It's not like they're saying a particular person committed a crime or something like that. This is a group of kids with no discernible reason for lying, more than one of which says she was there and more than one of which says she wasn't."

I nod. "Yeah. There's something off about it. I'm trying to track down pictures from that night. Hoping they will help clear up the confusion."

"'Less it ain't confusion," Merrill says, "and they just lying."

"In which case we'll have to find out why."

"Be hard to find out anything thirty-eight years later," Merrill says.

I shake my head. "Nearly impossible."

"You need help, you let me know," he says.

"What *are* you doin' with yourself these days?" Anna asks.

About three months ago, Merrill quit his job as a correctional officer because kids were getting killed by cops in the street and he wanted to make a difference.

"This and that," he says.

"Care to elaborate," she says.

"A little of this. A little of that."

"Oh, I see."

He laughs. "Fighting the good fight," he says. "Doing favors for friends. Helping out where I can."

"He's being vague out of modesty," I say. "He's volunteering at the Boys and Girls Club, he's in the Big Brothers Big Sisters program, he's helping raise money for the African-American Scholarship Fund, he's part of a program where he works with at-risk kids to build houses for seniors, and he's helping with some group I forget the name of now that's similar to the Innocence Project."

Finished eating and now yawning and rubbing her eyes with her tiny fists, Taylor is ready to be out of the highchair. Anna begins to put her in her carrier, but Merrill stops her.

"Let her sleep on Uncle Merrill's shoulder," he says.

"Sure."

Anna hands Taylor to Merrill, who props her on his muscular shoulder as if he's an old pro, and Taylor rests her small head near his neck and snuggles in to sleep as if it's how she falls asleep every night.

"And I thought you meant how was I payin' the bills," he says to Anna.

"How *are* you?" she says. "All that sounds like it pays in mansions in heaven."

"A little of this. A little of that. Odd jobs. Favors for friends. Track down shit that's missing—people, property, whatnot."

"So you're sort of like a Deep South Shaft?" she says.

"Who's the man who'll risk his neck for his brother man?" I say.

"Can you dig it?" Merrill says.

"Is that enough to make ends meet?" Anna says.

"First dollar I ever made, my mama made me put part of it up for a rainy day."

"'Cause your mama told you the same thing the Shirelles' mama told them?" Anna says.

"I've done that with every dollar I've ever made," he says. "Still doin' it. But it's there if I need it. Hell, y'all need a loan, just let me know."

Our food arrives—seafood platter for Merrill, grouper imperial for me, and honey-glazed salmon for Anna.

Anna and I both offer to take Taylor or to put her in her carrier, but Merrill tells us he only needs one hand to shovel the seafood into his mouth.

We eat in silence for a while, enjoying the evening and being together.

I finish first and ask them to excuse me for a moment. "I want to call Johanna before she goes to bed."

Walking down the wooden ramp to the beach below, I call my daughter at her mother's in Atlanta.

"Hey sweet girl," I say when I hear her soft, sleepy voice.

"Hey Daddy."

"How's my girl? How was your day?"

"I'm good. It was good."

"I miss you so much," I say.

"I miss you, Daddy."

I think about how similar our conversations are each evening and wonder how I can make them different.

"I can't wait to see you this weekend," I say. "We're going to have such a good time."

She doesn't say anything and I can hear her yawning.

"You sleepy baby?"

"Yes sir."

"Okay, I'll let you go so you can get some sleep. I love you so much. Sleep well. Sweet dreams. Night."

"Night, Daddy."

When I get back to the table, Merrill and Anna are talking about Ted Bundy.

"What makes the sheriff believe Bundy did it?" Merrill asks.

Like so many people in Pottersville, Merrill still refers to Dad as the sheriff. For an entire generation of us, he's the only one we've ever known.

"I'm not sure exactly. We're just starting. And I thought I was on vacation."

"You are," Anna says, patting my leg. "For a few more hours anyway."

"I was hoping to finish the murder book tonight and talk to Dad about it tomorrow. I know Bundy was in the area around the time Janet went missing and that she looked similar to his most common coed victim type, but I'd think it's more than that. Bundy being in the vicinity is enough to make him a suspect in a case like this, but Dad would have to have more than that to actually convince him he did it."

Chapter Twenty-three

It's late.

We're lying in bed reading—Anna, the new Zadie Smith novel, me, the murder book—propped on pillows, our bodies touching, the fingers of our hands not holding our books entwined.

"It's so good to see Merrill doing so well," she says.

I nod. "Unlike so many of us, he's not just talking about things, or worse, complaining about how bad things are, he's actually doing something about it, actually making the world a better place. Can't say that about many people."

"I wish he could find someone," she says. "Be as happy as us. It's the only thing missing from his life now. Wonder if Zadie Smith is single."

I laugh. "Now that'd be a good match."

"Don't you think he'd be even happier, do even more and better if he had someone?"

"He's about to find someone," I say. "Or she's gonna find him."

"You sound so certain."

"I am."

"Why do you think he is?"

"He's in the right places, doing the right things," I say. "It follows that's where he'll meet the right partner."

She nods. "You're right. Wonder if we could get Zadie Smith to come speak at a fundraiser for one of the organizations he's working for?"

I laugh and shake my head and keep reading.

After a little while, she yawns and closes her book.

"Any blood or physical evidence in the car that wasn't Janet's?" she asks.

I shake my head. "If there was, they missed it."

"Of course, Bundy rarely left any physical evidence behind, did he?"

"Not much, no. He was pretty meticulous."

"Is Bundy's DNA in the FBI database?" Anna asks.

"Not until just recently," I say. "Almost wasn't at all. Look at this. Dad stuck it in the book just a few years back."

I hand her the news clipping.

There's a national database of DNA profiles of convicts maintained by the FBI, but America's most notorious serial killer hasn't been a part of it until now.

Savage serial killer Ted Bundy, who confessed to murdering some thirty young women across several states before being executed in Florida's electric chair at Florida State Prison in Raiford in 1989, could now be proven to have committed many more.

Recently, a complete DNA profile of Bundy was created and is being submitted to the FBI database so that law enforcement agencies nationwide can finally determine whether Bundy was responsible for some of the open unsolved cases in their jurisdictions.

There has long been speculation that Bundy killed far more people than he confessed to. When one police interviewer asked Bundy if he had killed thirty-five woman, Bundy responded "Add a one to that." And now one of his former defense attorneys has a new book out claiming that Bundy confessed to him that he had murdered more than one hundred people.

The vast majority of murders ranged around the Northwest, but he traveled to Florida, continuing to kill young women, some very, very young, after escaping a Colorado jail at the end of December 1977.

After killing at least two women at Florida State University and brutally assaulting several others, Bundy then killed twelve-year-old Kimberly Diane Leach in Lake City before being captured on February 15, 1978.

Executed in 1989, Bundy was then cremated, which created a problem for police departments that later began searching for his DNA.

Following a few dead ends, investigators finally recovered a vial of Bundy's blood drawn in 1978 from a clerk's office in Columbia County—where he murdered the Leach girl.

Bundy's blood and the DNA profile it contains will now make its way to the FBI database so that investigators across the country might be able to now close several other cases.

The hunt to track down Bundy's DNA was primarily for the purposes of ascertaining whether or not Bundy was responsible for the death of eight-year-old Ann Marie Burr, the little girl many believe to be Bundy's very first victim.

It's interesting to note that a Florida law passed in 2009 requires police take DNA samples of all those arrested in felony cases.

Anna's not quite finished reading the article when my phone vibrates, and continues reading to herself as I answer it.

"Thought you were on vacation," Reggie says.

Reggie Summers is the sheriff of Gulf County and

my boss—at least one of them. I have a different one at Gulf Correctional where I'm a chaplain.

"I am," I say.

"From here and the prison?"

"Yeah?"

"Then why am I getting complaints from the sheriff of Jackson County that one of my investigators is harassing the fine folk up there?"

I think about who we talked to today, who might complain, and why.

"You there?" she says.

"Yeah, sorry. I was just thinking about it. Sorry you got the call."

"Glenn was cool about it," she says, referring to Glenn Barnes, the sheriff of Jackson County. "Just wanted to know what was going on and I couldn't tell him. So what's going on?"

"Dad is working one of his old cold cases and I'm helping him a little."

"Which case?"

I tell her.

"Why now?" she asks. "Is there new evidence or—"

"He's got the time now that he doesn't have a job," I say. "But he doesn't feel like he has much."

"Why's that?"

I tell her about his lab results and the bone marrow test and the fear that he has chronic lymphocytic leukemia.

For a long moment she doesn't say anything.

She doesn't talk about it much, but her mom has been sick—and in fact the reason she returned to Wewa was to care for her.

"I'm so sorry, John," she says, and I can tell she

means it. "Do what you need to do. Spend as much time with him as you can. Don't worry about things here. And if you need more time just let me know."

"Thank you, Sheriff. I really appreciate that. We're hoping the test comes back negative, which is a long shot, or that it's the highly treatable kind."

"I hope so too. My mom beat hers. It happens all the time. Just stay in touch and let me know if you need anything."

"Thank you."

"And the next time y'all are in Marianna, go by and see Glenn—as a courtesy and a favor to me."

"We had already planned to," I say, "but we'll do it first thing now."

Chapter Twenty-four

"So make the case for Bundy," I say.

I am driving Dad's truck. He is sitting awkwardly on his side in the passenger seat. We are driving along Highway 73 on our way to Marianna, the morning sun burning the dew off the pastures and pines.

"It's all circumstantial," he says, "but . . ."

Anna and Taylor are in her car in front of us—on their way to her parents' place in Dothan, which is about thirty miles above Marianna.

"Janet Lester looked an awful lot like Stephanie Brooks," he says. "Maybe as much as any of his victims."

He's right. She did.

Stephanie Brooks (again, not her real name) was the young woman Ted was in a relationship with in college who called it off—and became the pattern for the type of victim he was drawn to and preyed upon. Attractive. Straight, longish dark hair parted in the center.

Victim type, particularly for a serial killer, is highly significant, and Janet's similarities to Stephanie cannot be dismissed or downplayed.

"We know they both went to the Gulf station on 71 that night around the same time. So we have at least the possibility of a point in time and place where their paths intersected. A very good possibility."

I nod. "I want us to interview Little Larry again," I say. "But you're right. The fact that they both went to the same station around the same time that night is huge."

"The brutality and savagery of the crime," he says. "Not many people on the planet at the time are capable of a bloodletting like that."

It's not nearly as strong a point as the others he's made, but I understand why he's making it. And he's not wrong. Not many people are capable of such an extraordinary slaughter.

"The fact that he left no physical evidence," Dad says. "How many killers could do what was done to that poor girl inside her car and not leave a single drop of his own blood? Or hair? Or fibers? Or prints? That has Bundy all over it."

"That raises another point," I say. "I think we need to give some thought to how it was done. Because you're right, it seems impossible for there to be that much blood in such a small, enclosed space and there not to be a single piece of evidence."

He nods and seems to drift off in thought about it.

"I saw a note in the book that made reference to some other crimes committed that night," I say.

He nods. "Only one was possibly related, but we never found any connection. An old farm truck was stolen from the Carter's farm, which was not too far from the field where Janet's car was found."

"How far?"

He shrugs. "Couple of miles, I think."

"So Janet fakes her own death, leaves her car, steals the Carter's truck, and leaves town."

He shakes his head. "Truck didn't leave town. We found it back in town. Just parked on the side of the road. Nothing wrong with it. No damage. Not even much of the gas used. Most likely just a joyride, but it was close enough to the party, the field where the car was found, the Gulf station where Bundy was, to make me look into it and make a note about it in the book. We even tested it for prints but it had been wiped clean—which was suspicious but didn't tell us anything."

"I keep coming back to the possibility that it was staged," I say. "Either by Janet or someone else. The truck could be part of that. If someone stood outside the empty car and splashed buckets of blood inside it would explain why there is no evidence at all that a killer was ever in there with her."

He nods. "We looked at that possibility back then, but the ME said there were definitely signs of arterial spray, meaning her throat was slit in the car. Can't fake that."

I think about it. That certainly gives the greatest credence to the crime scene not being made to look like something it's not.

"We also have some of her prints in blood in the car," he adds. "So we know definitively that not only was someone attacked in the car, but that it was her."

I nod and think about it some more. There are many things that can be faked and or staged, but certain things just can't be.

"Back to Bundy," he says. "He often took his victims

with him."

"Yeah, but he usually abducted them in one location, killed them in another, then interfered with them in another."

"Interfered?"

I shrug. "Seemed better and shorter than saying 'played with and raped repeatedly.'"

"So this time, Bundy killed his victim in her car instead of his," he says. "Killed her as part of abducting her. Don't forget how much he had disintegrated by this point. He was no longer the suave predator luring coeds to his car. He was the vicious attacker of sleeping women in their beds and a child from her elementary school."

Anna's brake lights come on and I tap mine, searching the road in front of her to see if there's something in it, but it's just for a moment and she continues at the same speed.

I call her anyway.

"Everything okay up there?" I say.

"All good. How about back there? How's your dad feeling?"

"He's okay. Just a little tired and sore. But he must not be feeling too poorly. He's building a hell of a case against Bundy."

"I want to hear it tonight," she says. "Along with all the other details of your day."

"Just as soon as I hear yours."

"I can tell you mine now. Washed Mom's dishes. Cleaned her house. Cooked lunch. Hung out and listened to her and Dad tell me how pretty and perfect Taylor is."

"Save some of that cleaning for me," I say. "I'll try to get there early enough to help with things. I can also bring pizza or something for dinner. Don't forget you're still on vacation."

When I'm off the phone, Dad picks up right where he left off.

"The fact that we haven't found a body in all this time lets you know it wasn't an amateur. This guy knew what he was doing. No evidence. No body. No motive. How many other cold cases around the country right now are similar because Bundy did those too?"

"His closest biographers say at least ten but his defense attorney says over seventy."

"Either way this could be one of them," he says. "Then there's the Visqueen plastic with her blood on it. Have you gotten to that in the book?"

I shake my head.

"You will. It's in there. We found sheets of plastic with Janet's blood type on it up close to the interstate. I think Bundy wrapped her body in plastic to transport it and some of it fell out of his car when he was loading it or some of it blew out of the window when he was getting back on the interstate."

"No question it's possible," I say. "I can see why you—"

"I haven't even gotten to the best part yet," he says.

"Sorry. Thought that was all."

"Remember when Bundy was first arrested in Utah? Another time when a routine traffic violation got him pulled over. Utah Highway Patrol pulled him over in a Salt Lake City suburb."

I nod, trying to remember the details.

"The patrol officer saw that the Volkswagen's front passenger seat was missing, so he searched the car. Remember what he found?"

I do, but only vaguely. But it doesn't matter anyway. The question is rhetorical.

"A ski mask. Another mask made out of part of a pair of pantyhose. A crowbar. Handcuffs. Trash bags. Rope. An ice pick. Found what he thought was a burglary kit. But it was actually the kill kit of the most brutal bastard he would ever meet."

He pauses a moment and I glance over at him.

"In the woods bordering the pasture where Janet's car was abandoned we found similar items in a trash bag—and there were traces of Janet's blood both on items inside the bag and on the bag itself."

Chapter Twenty-five

Glenn Barnes looks like a small-town sheriff from a hit TV show. Young but not too young. Tall, muscular, tough, with a military-style haircut, slow, sincere manner, and clear but penetrating blue eyes.

He's polite, laid back, comfortable to be around.

He's cordial to me and respectful to Dad as he welcomes us into his office.

After an offer of coffee and a very small amount of small talk, we get down to it.

"I'm sure y'all understand the position I'm in here," he says. "Especially you, Sheriff Jordan."

"I not only understand it," Dad says, "I appreciate it, and don't want to do anything that causes you any aggravation or heartburn."

"I appreciate that. Now, let me give you the official line so we can get down to the real deal. Okay?"

We both nod, though mine is superfluous. He's only really looking at and talking to Dad.

"Anyone coming into our county and conducting any

kind of investigation is always told the same thing. You're free to do so as long as you don't interfere with any of our ongoing investigations, don't harass our citizens, and share anything you uncover with us."

"We understand," Dad says, "and don't have any intentions of doing anything else."

"Now, just between us," Barnes says. "I realize this was your case at one point. I also know that you two have a great deal of investigative experience between you. I also want this case cleared, and I don't care who does it."

He looks away a little, his blue eyes narrowing as the muscles in his jaw move beneath his tan skin.

"I knew her, you know," he says. "Janet. Wasn't in her grade. I was a year younger, but we had a couple of classes together over the years and my brother was in her class. She was a genuinely sweet girl. I wasn't at the party that night, but I've heard so much about it over the years sometimes it seems like I was. Her poor family. Hell, Ben's poor family. Hell, Ben himself. Sad, sad shit. I don't think he did it. Don't think he had anything to do with it, but he might as well have, the way his life turned out."

Dad and I are both quiet, waiting to see if he's going to say more.

Eventually, Dad says, "I don't care either. Who clears it I mean. We're not looking for credit or recognition. Just tryin' to lay to rest some ghosts—my own as much as Janet's. We'll turn everything we learn—*if* we learn anything— over to you. Let your department investigate and confirm everything for yourselves."

"I appreciate that, Sheriff," Barnes says. "And I'll tell you why. Our new DA is really pushing for results, pressing us to make an arrest. She wants Ben to stand trial, but

. . . unless there's something new uncovered, we've taken that case as far as it can go—and not just once but several times."

"Maybe we'll find something," Dad says. "But we do or we don't, we won't be getting in your way. And we'll turn everything over to you."

"Thank you," he says, standing. "That's all I ask. Now, I'll let y'all get to it. Know you didn't come up here to talk to me all day."

It feels like he's rushing us out, as if this was just a formality and now that it's done he's ready to be rid of us.

He and Dad shake hands and exchange a few more niceties.

"Who's your brother?" I say.

"Huh?" he says, turning toward me. "Oh. Brad. Brad Barnes. Why?"

"Was he at the party that night?"

He nods slowly, something in his eyes changing, as he studies me more closely now. "He was."

"What does he say?" I ask.

"About?"

"Any of it. Does he think Janet was there that night?"

He nods, seeming to relax a little. "Says she was definitely there. He saw her."

Chapter Twenty-six

When she wasn't crowned Miss Valentine queen, Kathy Moore wasn't shocked. She wasn't even surprised. But she was, at least a little, disappointed.

Janet always got everything, but she thought this time . . . just maybe . . . she might win something for once. After all, the judges were from out of town and didn't know any of them. They hadn't fallen under Janet's spell yet. They didn't know how sweet she was. How talented. How good. How she helped her mom with her brother. How she worked tirelessly at everything she did with a positive attitude. They didn't know how talented she was, how good at photography and fashion. So just maybe . . .

Kathy really thought she was totally blazin' and if there was ever a time for her, if she was ever going to beat Janet at anything, the Miss Valentine pageant was it, but no. Not even this. Not even at her best.

If someone had to win instead of her, she was happy it was her best friend. She really was. But did she have to

Bogart everything? Every. Single. Thing.

I mean, come on. Damnit man. Let me have something.

Most Talented. Most Attractive. Most Likely to Succeed. Best Dressed. Sweetest. The yearbook read like the bitchin' biography of Janet Leigh Lester.

Janet may have won everything so far, but Kathy had at least one more chance. Maybe, just maybe, she and Brad could beat Janet and Ben for Sweethearts' Ball king and queen.

It was a long shot, sure, but Ben brings Janet down a little and Brad brings Kathy up a little, and who knows?

Now she knew.

The ball was totally out of sight. Everything about it so groovy. It was as if they had been transported from their tiny little backwoods town to a totally bitchin' disco in a big city.

And everybody was diggin' her and Brad—the heads, the jocks, the nerds.

This could be it.

Ben seemed distracted and Janet far too worried about him to pay much attention to anyone else—all the students and teachers, each of whom represented a vote.

Creepy Clyde Wolf was staring at Janet again and something about it, about the way he had gotten even more freaky-deaky about it, not trying to hide it or anything, was making Janet and Ben even more la la.

If any night was her night, it was tonight. Even more so than the pageant. This was it.

But no. Not even when Ben and Janet were acting all dopey and bogus. Not even then.

Brad could tell how dejected she was. Told her he was sick of it. Said she needed to stop living in Janet's shadow. Told her to get her own life. It led to a big fight.

Kathy didn't think she was in Janet's shadow. They were friends. Best friends. They were in each other's shadows, right? This wasn't a one-way thing, was it? Had she been kidding herself? Did Janet see her as a fan instead of a friend?

No, come on. Cut it out. You know better. Janet is your friend. She's just what she seems. Y'all are just what you seem. But what do we seem to other people? Is Brad right?

Stick with what you know. You know Janet like a billion times better than Brad. You know that.

What she didn't know, what she still doesn't know to this day, was why after Janet was crowned queen for the second time in the same weekend, she hugged her a little longer than usual, a little too long, like she somehow knew it would be the last time she ever did.

Kathy meets us outside the administration building of Sunland Center, the community for individuals with intellectual and developmental disabilities. She is on her break.

She has aged well. She looks years younger than Sabrina, lightyears younger than Ben.

She's a modestly dressed middle-aged woman with light brownish hair going to coarse gray. Still shoulder length like it was back when she and Janet were best friends, parted in the center, but now pulled back into a ponytail.

She stands before us holding an expandable file folder in her right hand.

"I've gone over and over that night across the years," she says. "Haven't been able to shake anything loose by turning it around again and again in my mind. Not sure I can add anything."

The moment we stepped out of the air-conditioned truck, the sweat began to pour out of us, dampening our bodies, causing our clothes to cling to us. Kathy has led us over to the side beneath the shade of a huge oak tree, but even in its shade the heat and humidity are intense, and I'm worried about Dad, who seems to be moving even more slowly today.

I wonder why she doesn't meet with us inside one of the buildings, out of the heat, but decide not to ask until we're well into the interview, if at all.

"We understand," Dad says. "It's a long time ago now. Believe me, I know. But talking helps—helps us, and it may help you remember something that thinking about it alone won't."

She shrugs and turns up her lips, then nods. "Maybe so. I'd do anything to help. I still can't believe it happened. At times the wound is as fresh as if it happened yesterday. Others it feels like something that happened to other people—like in a story I heard or something. In the yearbook, Janet was most likely to succeed, not die. And God, do I feel bad for her family. They never got over it. You never do, though, do you? The death of a child. It's just not . . . You can't get over it. And probably don't want to."

"Do you have children?" I ask.

She shakes her head. "Never did. Looking back, I think it might be more because of what happened to Janet than anything else." She tilts her head back toward Sunland. "These are my children. I've tried to get Verna—Janet's mom—to put Ralphie out here. She can't really take care of him. She's always been a little frail."

Ralphie is Janet's little brother who was born with mental and physical impairments.

"Even got permission for him to come out with me during the day," she continues, "but she wouldn't even hear of that. Since Janet died, she clings to Ralphie like the last piece of floating wreckage of what once was her life."

"A poet," I say, nodding appreciatively. "Nice image."

She blushes a bit, a plume of red rising up her neck. "In my youth. Not anymore." She looks away wistfully, her eyes narrowing as if squinting to see something. "Time is a thief. Robs us of so much along the way then steals everything in the end. Hadn't thought of this in years—years and years, maybe decades. Janet and I were going to do a book together. Words and pictures. My verse, her photography."

"Maybe you still should," I say.

She looks as if the thought has never occurred to her, not in almost four decades.

Reaching over with her left hand, she's caressing the folder she's holding in her right. "Here are the pictures I promised," she says. "Hope they help. They're all I could find. Photocopies of pictures from the party that night, from school, from the ball and pageant that weekend, and, of course, several of Janet's. I'd almost forgotten how good she was. What an eye."

She squeezes the folder with both hands then hands it to me.

"Thank you. These are going to be extremely helpful."

The traffic on 71 is steady, lots of trucks, many of them towing livestock trailers. All of them seeming to be traveling way too fast.

"About the party that night," Dad says. "You still

certain you remember seeing her there?"

"I am. I wouldn't say it if I wasn't. She was this amazing, electric person. I'd've been aware of her even if she wasn't my best friend. She was there."

"Did you talk to her?" he says.

She shakes her head. "She never came inside. I'm not sure why exactly. I only saw her from the upstairs window. She didn't stay long. She pulled up. She and Ben talked for a little while, then he left with her."

"What were you doing upstairs?" he asks.

"I hope you won't think too badly of me if I tell you that my boyfriend and I had just made love. There was a bedroom up there with an old mattress on the floor. I shudder to think of how dirty it must have been now, but . . . He had gone down the hall to the bathroom and I was getting dressed near the window when I saw her pull up."

"We don't think badly of you at all," I say. "He was a very lucky young man. Brad Barnes, right?"

"Gosh, this is really going to sound bad, but . . . I was young and . . . he wasn't really my boyfriend . . . anyway . . . Brad broke up with me at the ball."

"Really? Wow. What a terrible thing to do."

"It really was," she says. "I was hurt and I was young and impulsive and . . . I had been drinking. I was up there with a guy named Gary Blaylock. It wasn't a one-night stand or anything. We dated for a long time after that, even lived together for a while after high school."

"He also saw Janet there, didn't he?" Dad says. "I didn't realize y'all were together."

"We weren't. I was in the bedroom. He was in the bathroom. We didn't know we'd both seen her 'til later."

"Why'd you and Brad break up?" I ask.

The color drains from her face, she takes a deep breath, and it appears as though it physically hurts her to say it. "He was hung up on Janet. He sensed something was wrong between her and Ben and he thought . . ."

Dad and I exchange a look she doesn't see.

"That never came out back then either," Dad says.

"Sorry. I was embarrassed, but I wasn't trying to hide anything. If I'd thought it had anything to do with what happened to Janet . . . I would've . . . said something, but . . ."

"It may have been the key to solving the whole thing," Dad says.

"*What?*" she asks, her voice rising. "How? I don't understand."

"What if Brad tried something and she shot him down and he lost it and . . ." I say. "What if she and Brad got together? What if Ben found them?"

"Oh my God. No. There's . . . no way. Believe me, I'm not fan of Brad Barnes but there's no way he or Ben could do what was done to Janet. Not in a millions years. No way. It has to be Bundy. Do something like that. Has to be. I just wish we knew where he hid her body."

Chapter Twenty-seven

"How are you holding up?" I ask.

Dad and I are back in his truck, driving away from Sunland.

"I'm okay."

"What do you need? You ready to eat? Need something to drink? Take something?"

"What I need is a new body," he says. "Short of that . . ."

"Figured we go see Janet's family now, then get some lunch, and I'll track down a few things while you take a nap."

He doesn't say anything. He's been resistant to the idea of going to see Janet's family, though he hasn't come out and said so, and I wonder what his hesitation is about.

"Do you not want to go see Janet's family?" I ask.

"We've got to see everybody," he says.

"You just seem hesitant to go there."

"It's a sad place," he says. "And a reminder of my

biggest fuckup and failure."

I nod slowly and give him an understanding look. "I can go alone if you'd rather."

"Nah. Thanks. I've got to face them again. Just . . . not looking forward to it."

"Then we should do it next and get it out of the way."

He nods. "Fine. What about what Kathy said?"

"Sheriff rushes us out of his office this morning and now we find out his brother had a thing for the victim and made a play for her the night she disappeared."

"Got to add him to our list of people to interview," he says. "But what about two of the main witnesses who say they saw Janet there that night and saw her leave with Ben having the kind of connection they do?"

"A love connection?"

"Angry, revengeful, I-just-got-dumped-because-my-boyfriend-has-a-thing-for-my-best-friend sex is not love," he says.

"You speaking from experience?"

Ignoring my question he asks one of his own. "Why not tell us they were together upstairs that night?"

"Maybe out of embarrassment. Like she said."

"Maybe," he says. "Or maybe they're lying. One saw from the bedroom window at the same time one saw from the bathroom window down the hall. You heard what Sabrina said. Kathy was obsessed with Janet. Was jealous of her, wanted to be her—or at least take her place."

"If it was someone Janet knew and not Bundy or another stranger," I say, "why take the body? Why hide it? Why do that to her family? Seems like an excessive level of hate and anger."

"Yes it does. And that's worth remembering."

We ride along in silence a moment, Dad trying to get comfortable in his seat.

"You heard from Jake?" I ask.

"No. Why?"

"I tried calling him last night and this morning and it goes straight to voicemail, which is full, and he hasn't called me back."

The Lester place is an old two-story wooden house on some former farmland. It sits at the end of a wooded, white rock and pebble driveway, an old barn where Janet used to keep her horse in the back. The yard, like the house and the barn and the family, is in disrepair, in need of care and restoration.

One look at Verna Lester and I can see why Dad was averse to the idea of coming here. She wears her bro-kenness like a burial shroud and the sadness in her eyes is difficult to take in, though I don't look away.

"*Jack*," she says to Dad when she opens the door, her voice filled with surprise and something else—more pain maybe, or maybe something a little more subtle and com-plex than that, something bittersweet with streaks of pain and pleasure.

"Verna," Dad says, taking off his hat and holding it in his hands. "Mind if we come in? This is my son, John."

"Hi John. It's so nice to meet you. Yes. Sorry. Please come in."

She leads us through a cathedral-ceilinged foyer filled with huge framed photographs, mostly professional portraits, of Janet and Ralphie, through an immaculate and nicely furnished open-concept living room/dining room/kitchen, to a den beyond.

Unlike the rest of the rooms, the den actually looks lived-in—a comfortable, well-worn couch and chairs, a TV showing cartoons, a small stack of mail that includes a newspaper and a couple of catalogs on the coffee table.

Ralphie, a soft, overweight man with glasses, hearing aids, and other obvious impairments, is seated in a recliner snickering and repeating certain words and lines from the cartoon on the television.

"Ralphie, you remember the sheriff," Verna says, muting the TV with the remote from the coffee table.

"Hey Ralphie," Dad says.

"Sheriff Jack," Ralphie exclaims, clearly happy to see Dad. "Sheriff Jack."

"*Hey*," Dad says. "How's my old crime-stopper buddy?"

Dad's demeanor and tone of voice take on a certain quality of kindly condescendence that is sweet and endearing.

Not only is this extra time with Dad such a gift, the opportunity to help him so rewarding, but I'm getting to see and appreciate him in ways I never have before.

With the help of a cane, Ralphie pushes himself up and awkwardly hugs Dad.

Ralphie is large and crippled, Dad weak and sore, and I step over toward them to catch Dad if Ralphie's weight and clumsiness is too much for him.

"He's always loved your dad," Verna says. "Sheriff Jack is his hero."

"Mine too," I say.

"Okay, Ralphie," she says. "Let him go now. Sit back down and I'll turn your show back up."

Slowly, reluctantly, Ralphie lets go and returns to his recliner.

I look over at Dad. He's breathing heavily but seems okay.

"Why don't we step out onto the porch so we can talk?" Verna says as she turns up the volume on Ralphie's cartoon.

"Let me know when you need my help to get the bad guys," Ralphie says. "I'll be ready, Sheriff Jack."

"Will do, Ralphie," Dad says. "Will do."

"Mama'll be right back here on the porch if you need me, baby," she says.

"I'm gonna go put on my supercool special crime-fighting uniform," Ralphie says.

"Okay. Come show it to us when you come back, okay?"

"Roger that," he says, and hurriedly hobbles out of the room and toward the back of the house.

Verna leads us through a set of French doors and out into a glassed-in Florida room where we sit on white wicker furniture with thick cushions.

"You okay, Jack?" she says, patting Dad's arm affectionately.

He nods.

The color has drained from his face and his breathing is labored.

"You sure?" I say.

"Yeah. Just need to catch my breath."

"Let me get you a glass of water," Verna says, pushing herself up and leaving the room.

"You really okay?" I ask.

He nods. "Just winded. It's hard for me to be back in this house. And I feel so bad for not staying in touch, especially with Ralphie. I . . . just . . . out of my own discomfort I stayed away."

Verna returns with a glass of water.

Beneath her life-long grief, there is an attractive, stately older woman. In glimpses, I can see the poised, even regal woman she would be if not for the shroud of sadness, the loss of faith and hope and joy.

Handing the glass to Dad, she rubs his shoulder, then touches his forehead with the back of her hand. "I think you may have a little bit of a fever," she says.

I wonder if her comfort and intimacy is merely maternal and she would treat anyone the same way, or is the result of the time they spent together back when Dad was working the case. Her concern, her attentiveness are clearly expressions of appreciation and affection.

"I'm fine," he says. "Stop making a fuss. Thank you for the water. Now sit down and relax."

She does, but not before slapping him on the shoulder. "Jack . . ." The slap and the use of his name express equal parts frustration and fondness.

How many hours had they spent together, grieving mother and the lawman here to find her daughter's killer and avenge her death?

When Verna sits down, the little lilt and light from when she had been interacting with Ralphie and Dad are gone and the dead-eyed, sallow-faced, too-soon old woman who had first opened the door to us is back.

A crime, particularly murder, always leaves far more

victims than is at first apparent.

Verna is as much a victim as Janet was—maybe even more so.

In some ways, some more obvious than others, everyone involved, both families—Janet's and Ben's—Dad, this entire small town, is in some sense a victim of this violent crime and will never fully recover. But no one more than Verna.

We'll never know exactly what happened to Janet. We won't know what her last hours, minutes, moments were like, not fully. And we don't know what happened, if anything, once her life here ended. We don't know what happens to those who are taken, but for those left behind, we do know. We witness the sort of half life they are left with, shadowed by grief and loss, dogged by death, both in the monotony of daily existence and the excruciating pain of memories and those moments where the absence of the dead is particularly acute, is a fate, if not far worse than death, a death all its own.

Janet died once. Verna has died a million times.

Would she still even be here if she hadn't had Ralphie to care for, to take care of?

Ralphie appears at the door in a too-small Zorro costume—complete with pressed-on mustache, ornate sword, and black mask.

"Zorro," Dad says. "One of my favorites."

"I'll be right in here if you need me, Sheriff Jack," he says, and disappears again.

Verna smiles. "You've always been so good with him, Jack," she says. "He doesn't get a lot of that from anyone but me. Thank you."

"How's Ronnie?" Dad asks.

She shakes her head. "Not good. Wasn't doing particularly good before the . . . But what happened to Janet crushed him as much as anyone . . . except maybe me. He lost his business. I guess you probably didn't know that, did you?"

"I'm so sorry to hear that. No, I didn't know. I should've stayed in touch more, Verna. I'm sorry."

"We almost lost our house, but he owned some property around town. We've had to sell it just to hang on, that and the little bit of disability we draw. Did you know they built a new high school?"

Dad nods, though it's clear he doesn't understand why she's asking. "Back in 2005, wasn't it?"

She nods. "That's when it opened. That was our land out on Caverns Road they built it on. I didn't want him selling it, but if he hadn't we'd've lost our house and no telling what else. That was a bad time. I guess all times have been bad. 'Cept maybe for a little while on a certain day back in '89. Other than that . . . they've all been bad."

Ted Bundy was executed on January 24, 1989. I assume that's the day she means.

"Where is Ronnie?" Dad asks.

She frowns and shakes her head. "He starts drinking pretty early these days. It's . . . so . . . sad . . . pathetic really—he's gotten so many DUIs he doesn't have a license anymore, so he rides a bike to his bar. Seventy-year-old man on a bicycle on his way to get wasted because life is too unbearable if he's not. It's absurd."

Dad shakes his head. "What did I abandon you to? I should have stayed."

"Ronnie was getting bad before Janet was killed," she says. "Drinking. Gambling. Lost a lot of money to the

139

wrong people. We had threats and . . . it was bad."

Dad says, "I should have finished the case, should have found who did it, should have—"

"How much difference you think that would've made?" she says.

He shrugs his bony old shoulders. "Some. Maybe. I . . ."

"We're gonna do our best to solve it now," I say. "That's why we're here."

They both look over at me as if they forgot I was in the room with them.

Then Verna looks back at Dad, a confused look on her face. "I thought you said Ted Bundy did it?"

"I believe he did, but I want to be sure. As sure as I can be. Want to make sure I didn't miss anything."

"Miss . . . anything?" she says very slowly. "Seriously? You told me it was Ted. I wrote him all those years. You told me it was him. I believed you. I . . ."

"I believed it was," he says. "Still do. I just want to be sure."

Tears form in her eyes and begin to stream down her cheeks. "It's never going to end, is it?"

"Verna, I—" Dad begins.

"I need you to go," she says. "I . . . can't . . . right now. I need to be alone."

"But—"

"Jack, I need you to go now," she says. "We can talk later, but right now I need to be alone."

"Okay," he says. "I'm so sorry. I didn't mean to . . . I'm just trying to . . . I'm . . ."

Chapter Twenty-eight

I drop Dad off at his hotel and drive to the sheriff's department.

Since I'll be staying in Dothan with Anna and her folks, Dad decided to get a room up here for the week, something that will help facilitate his need for rest and cut down on his time in the car.

While he naps, recuperating both physically and emotionally, I decide to talk to Glenn Barnes again.

I find him out in the lobby shooting the breeze with a few of his underlings.

"Hey, John," he says, as if he's happy but surprised to see me. "Didn't expect to see you again so soon."

"You got a minute?" I say.

"Sure. Come on in."

As we walk back to his office, he says, "Where's your dad?"

"Catchin' a little rest. Not feeling too well."

"Sorry to hear that," he says. "He's a good man.

Hope all this isn't too much for him."

"He's tough and resilient. He'll be okay. I just thought I'd run down a few things while he's resting."

We arrive at his office.

"Sure," he says as we sit down. "What can I do for you?"

"Three things if you will."

"I'll do what I can. What's the first?"

"Have you ever worked this case over the years or read the file?" I say.

He nods. "A few different times in a few different capacities. Why do you ask?"

"I just wondered what you thought," I say, "wanted your take on it."

His eyebrows shoot up and he cocks his head back a bit. "I really appreciate that, John. I do. Tell you what I think, and I hate to say it, but there are some cases that just go cold. And they stay cold. And I'm afraid this is one of 'em. I don't want it to be. And maybe I'm wrong. Hell, I hope I am. I really do. But this case is pushing forty years old. Hard to see it getting solved now if it hasn't already. Know what I mean?"

"I do," I say. "And you're probably right, but I hope we can figure it out and get some sort of peace for everyone involved. But as far as the case itself, do you have a theory or prime suspect?"

He shrugs. "I can see why they thought it was Bundy. Probably was. Problem is, whole damn thing is circumstantial. That's why I don't think we'll ever know for sure. If it wasn't Bundy . . . I don't know. I don't think Ben did it. Hell, I'd have a hard time thinkin' any of her friends could do it, but if one of 'em did it, I'd have to think it came

142

down to an altered state—drugs or alcohol from the party that night—that made him go crazy. Either way, Bundy or a boy from the party fucked up on bad drugs, is the act of a madman."

"The second thing is . . . I wondered how to get in touch with your brother. Someone said they thought they saw him talking to Janet the night of the party but I haven't been able to track him down."

No one had said they saw him talking to her, but I thought it was a nice touch to toss in.

"Brad? Brad is on the road a lot for work but should be back in town later in the week. I'll put you in touch with him the moment he returns. Hell, if you want to talk to him in person, face-to-face like, you can do it right here. I'll let y'all borrow an office or use an interview room."

"Thank you," I say. "I really appreciate that."

"No problem. I can't imagine he knows anything, but I know he'll be happy to help if he can. So what's the third?"

"I was wondering if there have been any other similar cases in this area either before or after what happened to Janet?"

"That's a great question. I don't think there have been. And there's no question that anything obvious would've stood out to us, but it's not a bad idea for us to take a look at all our unsolved cases and see. Tell you what I'll do, I'll have one of my investigators work on it and see if we come up with anything."

"Thank you. But I think it's important not to just look at the unsolved cases. Need to look at all of them, even the ones that were cleared."

"That's a good point. You're exactly right. We may

have caught the bastard and not even know it."

"Or," I say, "someone else could've been charged for another one this guy did."

"Oh shit. You're right. I didn't even think about that. Like I said, it's a long shot but I think it's good to look at all possibilities. Tell you what, I'll walk down and talk to Darlene about it right now. You can go with me if you want to."

Chapter Twenty-nine

Darlene Weatherly is built like a high school linebacker. She is a squat, muscular, powerful fireplug of a young woman.

"Got something I need your help with," Glenn says as we walk into her office.

"Sure, Sheriff. What's up?"

"This is John Jordan. He's an investigator with the Gulf County Sheriff's Department."

"Nice to meet you," she says, extending her hand.

Her hand is iron-hard, her grip a force of nature.

"He and his dad, Jack Jordan, the former sheriff of Potter County and the man who originally headed up the Janet Leigh Lester investigation, are taking another look at that case."

She nods appreciatively. "That's good. Someone needs to."

"John had an idea that I should've thought of," Glenn continues. "Would you go back through our homicides and missing persons and see if there are any before or after Janet that are similar in any way?"

"That is a good idea, John," she says. "Not just another pretty face, are you? Sure, Sheriff, I don't mind, but I think we'd know if there were any."

"Maybe we missed something," he says. "Or whoever here before us did."

"Everybody in this town is just so familiar with the case," she says, "there's no way it wouldn't've stood out."

"Yeah, you're probably right, but there's no reason not to check."

"No, there's not," she says, then lowering her voice, "unless I've got other shit on my plate that I don't have enough time to get to."

"What's that?"

"I said you're exactly right, boss. I'm on it. It's a long period of time, but it's a small county with not many homicides or missing persons, so it shouldn't take too long."

"John made another good point," Glenn says.

"Did he now?" she says, tilting her head back and considering me under raised eyebrows.

"Don't just look at unsolved cases," he says. "Look at all the cases. See if there are *any* that have *any* similarities at all."

She doesn't look happy about it, but she says, "Yes sir. Will do."

"As soon as you finish let me know," he says to her. Then to me, "I'll give you a call if we turn up anything."

"Thank you, Sheriff," I say. "I really appreciate it."

We shake hands—his is nowhere as powerful as Darlene's—and he leaves. I hang back to talk to Darlene for a moment.

"I appreciate you doing this," I say.

She nods, but says, "No need to thank me. I wasn't given a choice."

"Sorry about that. I wasn't trying to make more work for one person. I just . . . Can I help in any way?"

"It's not a problem. Got nothin' to do with you. I'd just like to be asked occasionally—or assigned something real. Like I said . . . being the only lesbian in the department has nothing to do with you."

I nod and frown. "I understand and I'm sorry it's like that, but this *is* something real. Very real. And it could be the thing that helps solve it."

"How likely is that?" she says. "But I'll give it my best. You don't have to worry about that."

"Can I ask another favor?"

She sighs and scratches her head. "Sure, John," she says, her voice full of false enthusiasm. "I'd really like that."

"Actually, it's two favors. Sorry. I just wondered if you'd pull anything that looks like it could be even remotely similar. Even the longest of long shots."

"I will, but I'm telling you there won't be any. What's the other?"

"We're not having any luck locating one of the witnesses from that night," I say. "Loner with a juvenile record named Clyde Wolf. He didn't go to the party, just watched it from the woods across the way. Could you help me locate him?"

"I can tell you exactly where he is," she says. "He's in prison. And you may want to take a closer look at him, because he's in there for stabbing his ex-wife."

Chapter Thirty

"I don't know what we could've done any differently," Ken Tillman is saying. "But I'd give almost anything for all of it to have turned out differently."

It's midafternoon and Ken Tillman is already drinking. A lot.

He has coarse, closely cropped gray hair, a deeply tanned, deeply lined face, and bright blue, bloodshot eyes. He's sitting in a folding canvas lawn chair out in front of his dilapidated trailer in a yard that is filled with junk—a couple of old cars on blocks, a random refrigerator, an old dryer, some rusting bicycles, small mountains of crushed aluminum beer cans.

He is smoking and drinking, which is how he fills most of his days.

We are seated across from him in rickety lawn chairs of our own between his trailer and an old, rotting wooden storage shed beneath the canopy of an enormous oak tree.

While we are here talking to him, Anna is making some calls to her previous coworkers in Classification for more information about Clyde Wolf.

"For that poor girl, of course," he says. "But after it happened, once she was gone, then at least for all of us. Hell, it's the reason I brought you in, Jack. Tryin' to save us from somethin' like what happened."

A gold chain shows in the wild spray of gray hairs springing forth from the top of his loose-fitting wife beater.

This sad, smelly, shiftless man used to be the chief law enforcement officer of this entire county because a majority of the population here thought he should be. He was once respected and admired. He was once athletic and attractive.

The ripples of violent crime, of murder, seem to never end. Here is another life capsized by the wake of what happened to one girl on one night nearly forty years ago. Except it didn't just happen to one girl on one night, but to all involved, night after night—every night since the initial crime was committed.

"If we could've done anything else, I wish I knew what it was," he says. "Wish I could go back and do it."

A silver bracelet moves up and down his right wrist every time he drinks from his tall glass of whiskey, which is often.

"Ruined all of our lives," he says. "Ben and me have no life. Sent Mary, his mom, to an early grave. She's like Janet there. Got off lucky compared to the rest of us."

Though we are beneath the shade of an oak tree, the heat from the hot August sun is still stifling, the humidity hovering around a hundred percent, and the ice in Ken's whiskey looks like the polar icecaps filmed with time-lapse photography techniques.

"Y'all sure y'all don't want a drink?" he says.

We both nod.

"Thanks, but we're okay," Dad says.

"Look at us, Jack," Ken says. "We've gotten old as fuck. The hell that happen?"

Dad shakes his old head slowly, sadly.

And once again I think of the Mellencamp line, perhaps the truest he ever penned. *I know time holds the winning hand. I can tell by the lines on our faces.*

"Hell, it's not like our sons are young," Ken says, cutting his eyes over at me. "Though yours is younger than mine—and faring a hell of a lot better. Be grateful for that, Jack. Be . . . very . . . Count your blessings, man. It's a rough, raggedy-ass world. Chews us all up like we're mulch. You seen my boy yet?"

Dad nods.

"He's sadder 'n I am. And that's . . . sayin' somethin'."

Tears well up in his blue, bloodshot eyes.

"He lives in a tent. A fuckin' tent. 'Course he may have anyway. Always loved camping—in the backyard, in the woods. Always rather stay in a tent than . . . But if Janet hadn't been . . . If they had stayed together . . . they'd have a house. He wouldn't be so . . ."

He shakes his head slowly, looks down at the whiskey he's drowning in.

His life and that of everyone he loves has been decimated. Violent crime is like a category five hurricane hitting the coast, utterly and mercilessly catastrophic.

We are quiet for a long, pain-filled moment.

"Can't believe you're still tryin' to solve the damn thing, Jack," Ken says. "I really can't. I mean, goddamn, don't you ever give up?"

"That's the thing, Ken," Dad says. "I did. I shouldn't have, but I did. And I can't live with that."

"Oh, you'd be surprised at what you can live with," Ken says.

"You thought of anything over the years that we should've done that we didn't?" Dad asks. "Anyone we should've looked at that we didn't—or not close enough."

Ken shakes his head, then takes another long draw on his cigarette and pull on his drink. "Not a damn thing. I think we did all we could back then. I know my boy didn't do it. I think it's a safe bet Bundy did. It's just . . . one of those things. Sometimes you can do all you can and life still fucks you in the ass. And there ain't a thing you can do about it. Not . . . a . . . dang . . . thang."

"If it wasn't Bundy . . ." I say.

He shakes his head. "Everybody still believes it was my boy, that I covered it up, that your dad helped me, but . . . I swear to God on my boy's life I didn't. And Jack'll tell you he didn't cover anything up. We just didn't. I've heard 'em say that we planted the bag in the woods to make it look like it was Bundy."

It's a possibility I had wondered about myself—not that Dad had done it, but I've wondered if Bundy *wasn't* responsible, if the killer could have tried to make it look like he was.

Dad shakes his head. "People are so stupid."

"Do I fit in the category?" I say.

Dad looks at me.

"I don't believe you did it, but I have wondered if it was done by someone. The killer, maybe."

"It's absolutely impossible for anyone to have," Dad says.

151

"Why's that?"

"When Janet was killed, no one knew Bundy was responsible for Chi Omega or Kimberly Leach and no one had any damn idea Bundy was driving down I-10 from Tallahassee to Pensacola. Hell, they didn't know who he was when they arrested him or for a day or so after he was in custody."

I nod. "Sometimes people are stupid," I say. "Sometimes they just don't have all the facts."

They both smile.

"That's the biggest reason I believe it was Bundy," Dad says. "That kit found in the woods that had her blood on it. Always thought it had to be Bundy because no one else would even know to try to make it look like him. I think the Visqueen found near the interstate with traces of her blood on it also supports it being Bundy."

Ken nods. "We got as close to closing this one as we could," he says. "Only two things missing are Janet's remains and Bundy's confession. And I'll be honest with you, I don't think we're ever gonna get either of them. Bundy's dead, and with him any hope of finding her."

Chapter Thirty-one

Dad is quiet and looks to be in pain.

We are back in the truck, leaving the sad little corner of purgatory Ken calls home.

"You okay?" I ask.

He shakes his head.

"What is it? Do you need to—"

"I can't believe that's Ken Tillman," he says. "I can't believe how he's living."

I nod.

"How . . . everyone we've talked to is. The grief. The loss. The . . ."

"Hollowness?" I offer. "Desperation? Disintegration?"

Thoreau's line comes to mind. *Most men lead lives of quiet desperation and go to the grave with the song still in them.*

"I'm a foolish old man," Dad says.

I glance over at him. I've never heard him say anything quite like that before.

"I'm throwing effort after foolishness in some vain attempt at redemption or . . . And I've pulled you into it."

"I'm happy to be here," I say. "I think what we're doing is worthwhile."

"Ken's right. Glenn's right. They're all right. It's too late. I'm trying to . . . fix something before I die that—"

"There's nothing wrong with that."

We enter the historic downtown district and in many ways it's like driving back in time—a small Southern town with a vibrant main street of restored old buildings, a quaint quality exuding rural charm.

"I had my chance. I failed to do it when I might actually have been able to. Now I'm just wasting everybody's time. Just . . ."

I'm sure Dad has been critical of himself before. He may have even expressed it to someone, but not to me, not like this. I've never heard him be as open and vulnerable and emotionally honest as he is in this moment.

We continue past the old St. Luke's Episcopal Church and cemetery that played such a pivotal role in the Civil War battle here in 1864, and a series of big, beautiful and beautifully restored antebellum homes.

"The time to close the case was when I had the chance, when there were still leads and witnesses who re-membered what happened and . . . Not when it's gone cold. Hell, that's the understatement of the day. It's four decades cold. Hard to imagine a case any colder."

"Then you're not trying," I say. "Zodiac. Jack the Ripper. Cain and Able."

"I'm serious."

"I am too. 'Cept for the Cain and Able bit. Figured a little levity might not hurt."

Driving through Marianna, I'm reminded just how much beauty and charm is present here, and I wonder again how so many truly terrible and tragic events could've happened here—the torture and lynching of Claude Neal, the horrors that happened at Dozier School for Boys, the savage murder of Janet Leigh Lester.

"Look at the shape all these people are in," he says. "The condition of their lives. All of them. Not just Ken, but Ben and Verna and Ronnie and Kathy. And it's at least partly because I didn't do my job. I . . . I not only didn't finish the task I was assigned, I . . . left and never looked back. All these years I kept telling myself I'd come back and solve it one day, but even when I was lying to myself about that, I never once thought about these poor people, never imagined for one moment they could be suffering to the extent they are because I fucked up. Because I failed them."

"I appreciate how you're feeling," I say. "I do. And I get it. I'd probably feel the same way. But you took the case as far as it would go and that's all you could do."

"But I didn't."

"Whatta you mean? I thought you did."

"I left before it was done. I . . . It doesn't matter. Take me back to the hotel. I'm done."

"But—"

"Go be with your family. Don't waste any more time on this. Enjoy your vacation. I should've never asked you to help clean up my mess. I'm sorry I did."

"You're just feeling—"

"I'm done talkin' about it," he says.

And he is.

I continue to try to get him to talk for a while, but

it's futile.

If we had a different type of relationship, if we were closer, if we were less like distant father and son and more like adult friends, more like intimate peers, I could have insisted that he talk to me, that he let me help process what he's dealing with and going through.

As it is, we are family but we are not close, intimate, peer-like friends. I don't doubt Dad's love, respect, and support. In fact, I know he'd do anything for me—anything but let me help him on any kind of emotional or psychological level. He'll let me help him work the case but not with his inner life of thoughts and feelings. Our dynamic, the one he established when I was a child and continues to insist on to this day, is one that avoids the true intimacy that comes from shared vulnerability.

Chapter Thirty-two

After dropping Dad off, I search for a quiet place to go through the folder of pictures Kathy had given us.

I feel bad for Dad, and wanted to stay to talk to him, but he insisted that he needed to be alone and wanted to sleep. I reluctantly acquiesced but told him I'd check on him a little later and that Anna and I would bring him some supper.

I drive down Caverns Road to Citizens Lodge Park and sit in a gazebo by a lake and spread the pictures out before me.

The disparate images range from poorly lit and poorly shot and poorly developed pictures from the night of the party, to the artistic photography of Janet Lester.

The snapshots from the party are dim and blurry, but show much of what the witnesses have described. Kids in late-seventies attire hanging out, drinking, dancing, makin' out, mackin' and mean muggin' for the camera.

Janet is not in a single picture from inside the farmhouse, though Ben is in several—as are Kathy and Charles Fountain and Valarie Weston and Gary Blaylock.

There are no shots of Sabrina Henry, which I find strange.

The only image that appears to have Janet in it makes her look like an apparition accidentally imprisoned on film as the photographer attempted to capture something else.

Turning toward her car, seen in profile, a twirl of light. Cream crinkled-texture blouse, lace yoke. Camel, tan, and rust floral-print skirt, deep flounce at the bottom.

Eerie. Ethereal. Evanescent.

The picture was taken from inside the farmhouse, a glare from the glass window creating a frame in the foreground and adding an odd light to the entire image.

Behind the swirl of floral print and light, her red Mercury Monarch appears possessed like a chariot from hell.

Later, Anna picks me up and we head to Tallahassee to see Sam Michaels.

We are in her Mustang GT on I-10, taking the same route as Bundy had the night of Janet's death, only in reverse. She is driving while I look at Kathy's photographs and murder book.

Anna has spent the day caring for her mother, helping around her house, and is as happy as I am to be able to get away together for the evening.

It is doing little things like this together, these seemingly inconsequential, average, mundane activities, that makes life so much sweeter, richer, and fuller. Just being together, being partners in all things.

Ordinary life in the company of an extraordinary woman is anything but.

"How's your mom?" I ask. "How are things up their way?"

"She's okay. Not as incapacitated as we were led to believe. I really think it just came down to Dad wasn't babying her quite the way she wanted and she was disappointed about missing our vacation and wanted to see us. But she's doing well enough I had no problem leaving Taylor with them tonight. How's your dad?" she asks. "The case."

I tell her.

"So is that it?" she asks. "Y'all stopping the investigation? The fact that you're looking at those pictures and the murder book suggests otherwise."

I smile. "I'm not stopping. I don't think he really is either. I bet by morning he'll be back on the scent and we'll pick up right where we left off."

She shakes her head and frowns. "It's gotta be so hard for him. To see just how wounded all these people are and to feel responsible in some way."

"Yeah."

"And I hate to think of him alone in that hotel room. You told him we'd love to have him at the 'rents place in Dothan?"

I nod. "He really wants to be alone, but I'll keep tryin'."

She glances at the photographs in my lap.

"Anything helpful?" she asks.

"Maybe. It's definitely good to have a context and some visuals. Certainly feel like I know and understand

Janet even more. She had an amazing eye—particularly for portraits."

"Any evidence she was at the party?" she says.

"Yeah. Look at this."

I hand her the picture. She holds it up above the steering wheel and glances back and forth between it and the road.

"Wow. Haunting."

"When I called Kathy to talk to her about it she said it had always spooked her, said maybe Janet wasn't at the party that night after all, only her ghost after she was killed."

"It is uncanny," she says, handing the picture back to me without taking her eyes off the road. "Especially given what happened to her that night."

Chapter Thirty-three

Sam Michaels and Daniel Davis live in an old two-story wooden home on a small hill in a heavily wooded lot in Tallahassee.

Daniel was once a religion professor and ritualistic crimes consultant. Sam was a special agent with the Florida Department of Law Enforcement. Now Daniel is a full-time caregiver; Sam, the one he's giving care to.

Sam, who I had worked with on a serial case back in the spring, suffered a brain injury as the result of being shot at point-blank range. For a while, her doctors believed she wouldn't wake up from the coma she was in, but not only did she do that, she's undergoing mental and physical rehabilitation and making progress—none of which came as any surprise to anyone who knows Sam.

The high-ceilinged, hardwood-floored living room of their home has been converted into a recovery room. Couch and coffee table removed, a hospital bed has been placed in front of the empty charred fireplace. Beside it, a single chair for Daniel is the only other piece of furniture in the room.

The hardwood floors creek as Daniel leads us into the room, and Sam opens her eyes, turns her head slightly, and looks up at us.

"She's having a good day," Daniel says.

Sam's eyes widen and flicker with recognition as a smile plays on her lips.

"Hey, partner," I say. "How's it going?"

"You look so good," Anna says.

Sam smiles wider and nods her head ever so slightly.

Every time we see her she's getting better and doing more.

"You're doing so well," I say. "You'll be trackin' down bad guys again in no time at all."

She tries to nod again.

"I heard the FDLE case clearance rate has plummeted since you've been sidelined," Anna says. "They need you back as soon as possible."

Daniel, who is out of Sam's sightline, has tears in his eyes, and I can't tell if they're tears of sadness or happiness, but can't imagine they're not both.

He looks pale and exhausted, the ends of him frayed like an old rug.

"So here's what we're gonna do," Anna says. "I'm gonna sit down here beside Sam for some girl talk. Daniel, you're going to give John a list of everything you need. I mean everything—from toilet paper to tea bags—and while John is shopping and picking up a delicious dinner from Ted's for us, you're going upstairs and taking a nap."

And that's exactly what we do—except while I am out, in between picking up household items for Daniel and

Sam and grabbing dinner at Ted's Montana Grill, I drive around the area where Ted Bundy lived and took lives while he was here—including Chez Pierre, Chi Omega, and where his rooming house, The Oak, had once been.

Jack Jordan reenters his hotel room after going out for some food and a walk. Though he had rested and napped earlier when John had dropped him off, he's still drained and depressed. Maybe even more so now.

The room is dark and cool. The drapes are drawn and the only light is a narrow strip coming from the slightly ajar bathroom door.

Kicking off his boots, tossing his hat on the chair in the corner, and emptying his pockets on the bedside table, he collapses on top of the covers with all his clothes still on.

The room smells the way most hotels do—of commercial cleaners and air fresheners, of emptiness and stillness and staleness, of a running window unit, and of previous guests, some of whom had broken both federal and state laws and had smoked in here. And not just cigarettes.

Given his fatigue and depression, given the multilayered smells in the room, given his advanced years and compromised health, it's little wonder he neither sensed nor smelled that there was somebody already present when he had entered the room.

He wants to sleep, to succumb to the safety of unconscious oblivion, but all he can think about is Verna and Ken and Kathy and Ben and how damn depressing their lives are, about Janet and how her death and disappearance go unavenged all these years later.

Guilt. Failure. Regret. Pain.

He feels his own pain, of course, but it's their pain that he finds overwhelming.

Did Bundy really do it? How can he prove it if he did? Where is her body? How can he find it now?

The pasture and pond where her car had been found and the woods surrounding them had been thoroughly searched back then, but the only thing they discovered was the bag with the kill kit.

Where could she be?

If he took her with him, her remains could be scattered over several counties west of here or—that's it. Wow. Why hasn't he thought of that before? That's got to be it. That's where she is.

On his way from Tallahassee to Pensacola, Bundy had gotten the stolen VW he was in stuck in a restricted area of Eglin Air Force Base—and had only gotten it out with the help of a service station attendant. It has always been believed that Bundy was there hiding out, but what if he was there to bury Janet's body? He often took his victims to secluded places in the woods to do all kinds of disturbing things to them—including necrophilia. What if that's what he was there for? What if wasn't hiding out, but defiling and discarding Janet's body? That's it—or could be. Certainly makes more sense than any other theory he's ever come up with. They already know that Bundy used the area to throw away several personal items and the VW's passenger seat. What if he threw out the seat and other things because they had Janet's blood on them?

Jack has a jolt of energy and excitement he hasn't had in a very long time.

He starts to sit up to call John, but just as he's about

to someone is there on top of him, pinning him down, pressing a gun into his forehead.

Where is my gun?

If have to ask that question it's time to hang it up.

I came in. Dropped everything on the bedside table. Is that where it is?

He can't remember placing the gun on the table.

I am in bad shape.

The truth is he's old and sick and retired, but even before that, he hadn't had to pull his gun many times over his decades in law enforcement. Still, he always knew where it was.

The guy on top of him now is in all black—including gloves and a ski mask.

"Listen up and you won't get hurt," he says.

Jack makes a small nodding gesture.

"Good people in this town. Don't need you digging up bad memories for them. Understand?"

The man's voice comes out in a low, harsh, growling whisper. Utterly unrecognizable.

"Let sleepin' dogs lie. Leave the ghosts alone. No good'll come from stirring all this horrible shit back up."

Jack still doesn't respond.

"Nod if you understand me."

Jack doesn't nod.

"Something you need to know. I won't let you keep bothering people I care about. I'll take you off the board first. I will. What's another? You act like you're already knockin' on death's door. Keep doin' what you're doin' and I'll open her up for you."

The man climbs off Jack to stand beside the bed.

As he does, Jack reaches for his gun on the nightstand—only to find it's not there.

"Way ahead of you, old man," he says. "It's my gun now."

He presses the barrel of the gun back into his forehead.

"I can see you learn as slow as you move," he says. "Should shoot right here and now. But I'm gonna give you one more chance. But that's it. One more. Stop what you're doin' and go home or . . . there won't be any other warnings, no other chances. This is it. Do what I tell you or you won't even know there'll be a next visit. You'll just be breathing, and then you won't."

Chapter Thirty-four

"Are you really okay?" Anna asks Dad.

"I'm fine. Only thing he hurt was my pride."

We are in Dad's room, having gotten a call from him about what happened on our drive back from Tallahassee.

He is sitting up, leaning back against the headboard. I am standing at the end of the bed. Anna is sitting on the edge of the bed between us.

"No idea who it was?" I ask.

He shakes his head.

"Of the people we've talked to," I say, "who'd be the closest in size, shape, weight?"

He shrugs. "Really have no idea."

I nod. "I called Merrill and Jake on the way here," I say.

"Why?"

"For a little backup. Reinforcements."

"Jake?"

"When Merrill said he just couldn't get away from what he was working on."

"Oh."

"But he didn't answer."

"Don't need backup," he says.

"I'm assuming we're stickin' with it," I say.

"I won't be scared off anything," he says, and I know he means it, but it sounds a little like hollow bravado.

"I meant because of what you were saying when I dropped you off this afternoon."

"Oh. Yeah, well . . . Sorry about that. I was already over that when the little punk jumped on top of me, but I was twice as over it by the time he left. I was already back working on the case. I'd had this idea about where Bundy may have hidden Janet's body when the little cat burglar–looking bastard came in and ripped it all to shreds."

"Why ripped it to shreds?" Anna says.

"Because," I say, "if Bundy did it why would some-one—anyone—come in here and threaten Dad off the case."

"Exactly," he says.

"Unless," I say, "the guy has something else to hide—something we might uncover if we keep picking at this particular scab. What was your thought about Bundy?"

"Remember he got his VW stuck in Eglin? What if he was there to bury Janet's body? They found some of his stuff and the passenger seat of the car. What if her body was somewhere else around there and that's why it's never been found?"

I nod. "That's good. Very good. Need to get them to check it out."

"The old brain still fires up and runs occasionally,"

he says.

"For tonight, you can come back to Anna's parents' place with us and—"

He shakes his head. "I don't need babysitting. Don't need Merrill or Jake to come here. Don't need to go there with y'all."

"It's not babysitting," I say. "It's—"

"I'll tell you what it is," he says. "It's nonnegotiable. I won't be scared away and I won't be babysat. Only thing I need is the loan of a gun. Bastard took mine."

"But—"

"That's the end of it," he says. "I'm done talking about it. Besides, he threatened me. Said if I didn't do what he told me he'd be back. I want to be where he can find me when he comes back. And I intend to get some information out of him."

"Then John will stay with you," Anna says. "And that's nonnegotiable."

He shrugs and considers it. "We could sleep in shifts."

I nod, then look at Anna. "Are you sure?"

"Positive."

"Thank you."

"Y'all are also going to call Glenn Barnes and let him know what's going on," she says. "Get him to have his department keep an eye out for y'all too."

"What if it was him?" Dad says. "Or he's behind it?"

"Do you think it was him?" I ask. "He's a big guy. Was—"

"Nah, wasn't that big, but he could be behind it. Ben. Brad. Clyde. Gary. One of the other girls like Sabrina or Kathy. Anybody could be behind it."

"Including Janet," Anna says. "What if she faked her death and is scared you're going to find out? She could've sent someone to threaten you."

Dad frowns and shakes his head. "ME said there was too much blood in her car for her to have survived."

"Unless it wasn't her blood," Anna says. "Could've been someone else's. Maybe that's why she had him threaten you off. She killed someone else and doesn't want it discovered."

"Who?" Dad says. "There were no other missing persons around that time. And the blood in the car was her rare type."

She shrugs. "I don't know. Maybe they weren't from around here. Or maybe there wasn't a victim at all. Maybe she robbed a blood bank or saved her own blood over a long period of time. Maybe her stepdad was molesting her and she wanted out and so she—"

"There's just no evidence of any of that," Dad says. "I looked into all that. It's possible. Most things are—at least in theory until we find her remains or other evidence. But you're right, we certainly need to keep it in mind as a possibility like all the others until we can narrow things down even more."

"And if she didn't fake her own death to get away from her stepdad, maybe it was her stepdad who killed her," she says. "Maybe he's the one who came over here and threatened you—or sent someone to do it."

"We'll be sure to ask him when we talk to him tomorrow," Dad says.

Chapter Thirty-five

"I owe you both an apology," Verna says. "I acted badly and I'm very sorry. I don't handle things as well as I once did. Still a little fragile. I hope you can forgive me. It just took me by surprise. All this time . . . I thought Ted Bundy killed my baby . . . and if he didn't . . . well . . . anyway. I hope it goes without saying that I appreciate what you're doing and want to help in any way I can. If Bundy didn't take Janet from us, then I want to know who did, and if he did, then I want to know where she is and to have the opportunity to bring her home and bury her in a sacred place."

"We understand," Dad says.

"Absolutely," I say.

We are in her house once again—at her invitation—after having spent the morning working with Glenn Barnes and Reggie Summers and a few other law enforcement individuals and agencies to coordinate with Eglin Air Force

Base for a search of Janet's remains in the area where Bundy was known to be.

Ralphie, in a complete Batman costume, is in his chair watching Batman on TV. The only part of him visible is the bottom half of his face beneath his cowl.

Ronnie is already at the bar.

We are with Verna around the island in her kitchen drinking sweet iced tea.

"Thank you. I really felt bad. I'm so relieved y'all forgive me. So now that I'm in a better place . . . how can I help?"

"You mentioned corresponding with Bundy," I say.

"Yeah, that was part of what upset me so bad, because I spent all those years writing that monster trying to convince him to confess and to let us know where he hid my baby. If he didn't do it . . . well . . . what a waste of time that was."

"We all spent a lot of time trying to get him to confess," Dad says, "trying to get him to tell us where to find her. I had three different interviewers try to get it out of him over the years. I even tried to get in to talk to him myself before he was executed, but he refused to talk to me—or anyone else except James Dobson."

Just prior to his execution, Bundy, manipulative madman to the end, granted his final interview to conservative Christian radio talk show host and psychologist James Dobson, in which the two famously talked about pornography as a root cause for his multiple assaults, murders, rapes, and necrophilia.

"Did he write back?" I ask. "What'd he say?"

"I wrote him for years," she says. "Lots and lots of letters, asking him not only to confess to Janet's murder and to tell us where he buried her, but to confess to every murder he'd ever committed so all the families could . . . would know. In all that time, I got one sentence from him. One sentence on a partial piece of paper that read, 'I'm not the monster you seek. Ted.' That was it."

"I got nowhere either," Dad says. "He did talk to a few interviewers about his crimes—usually in the third person or in some very vague ways, but not much about victims that weren't already known."

"I noticed there are no bars in Marianna," I say. "Where does Ronnie go to drink?"

She frowns and shakes her head. "It's so pathetic. It's a guy's basement. Decorated just like a bar—neon lights, pool table, dartboard, jukebox, lighted liquor shelves behind an actual wooden bar. It's . . . sad and . . . absurd, but . . . I'm just glad to have him gone. I know that sounds ter—"

"Batmom," Ralphie says from the den, "Batman need a Batsnack."

"Coming up, sweetie," she says, jumping up and beginning to prepare his food.

"Not sweetie," he says. "*Batman.*"

"Sorry, Batman. That's what I meant. Batsnack coming right up. Will be in the Batcave in no time."

She fills a Batman thermos with a purple drink from a pitcher and prepares mini grilled cheese sandwiches in the shape of bats.

"Feel free to keep talking," she says. "This will only take a minute."

While Dad asks her if she minds if I see Janet's room, I glance around the formal living room across from us that looks to never be used. Huge framed portraits and photographs hang on every wall. Based on the others I've seen, I'd say they're all Janet's work.

Happier times. Ronnie and Verna together, genuine smiles, comfortable affection. Ralphie in various costumes and crime-fighting poses.

A stunning self-portrait of Janet wearing an outfit not dissimilar to the one she was seen in at the party the night of her disappearance, a vintage remote-shutter-release trigger and cable visible in her left hand. All the images are great, are art, but the one of Janet is truly extraordinary, as if by being both photographer and subject simultaneously she is able to open herself up, expose her naked, vulnerable essence in a way she never could otherwise.

I step over to take a closer look at it, studying it carefully.

There is beauty—simple, pure, innocent beauty—but it's the openness and vulnerability that make the photograph so powerful and a little difficult to look at.

I feel as though I can see straight through her big brown eyes into her soul.

Is there pain present? Is this someone being molested by her stepfather? Is this someone capable of faking her own death? Of killing someone else? I honestly don't believe it is. I don't see anything in her—as art or artist—that would suggest anything even remotely like that.

When I return to the kitchen area, Dad is standing and Verna is next to him. Something about the way they stand, the way they lean into each other just a little makes it look like they were once lovers.

"We're going to Janet's room, Batman," she yells into the den. "We'll be right back."

"No," Ralphie yells. "My room. See my room first."

174

"Okay. We can see yours first. Do you want to show them or do you want me to do it?"

In another few moments, a large, old, overweight Batman is easing through the doorway with the aid of his Batcane.

"To the Batcave," he says, which is comical given how slowly he's moving.

When he's sufficiently in front of us, we follow.

"He's almost always a comic crime stopper," she says. "Ironman, Spiderman, the Hulk, but Batman is his favorite."

He leads us down a hallway lined with bookshelves.

"Ronnie used to read," Verna explains.

The books lining the shelves represent a diverse collection of fiction and history and philosophy and true crime and religion and self-help, with several shelves of farming and farming machinery mixed in.

"He doesn't do anything but drink these days," she says. "Not that I blame him. If I didn't have Ralphie to take care of that's probably what I would do. I haven't been able to read—or concentrate on anything for very long since it happened."

Ralphie's room is absolutely packed with collectables—toys, sneakers, figurines, lunch boxes, movie memorabilia, canes, old records, and antiques of all kinds, including tractors, swords, nunchucks, and, of course, comic books—all in pristine packages displayed as if in a showroom instead of a bedroom.

"Wow," I say. "This is very impressive."

"Ralphie throws himself into everything he does, don't you buddy?"

"I'm not buddy. I'm Batman."

"Sorry, Batman. Okay. We're gonna go look at Janet's room now. We miss Janet, don't we?"

"So bad," he says. "Miss her so bad. Janet is my sister. Janet takes pretty pictures."

"Yes, she does," she says.

They both use the present tense, and I wonder why. Is it just because of Ralphie's child-likeness or how much of Janet is still present in this house, or is there some other reason?

"You go watch more of your adventures, Batman," Verna says. "We'll be back in there in a minute."

"I love your room," I say. "It's very cool."

"Yes, it is. Coolest room ever. Coolest room ever, isn't it? Isn't it the coolest room ever?"

"Yes, it is."

As Batman slowly makes his way back toward the den, we turn to Janet's room.

Chapter Thirty-six

"It's just as she left it," Verna says. "Still. I dust and vacuum once a week without disturbing anything. Like before, I just ask that you don't move anything, don't change anything."

"We won't," Dad says.

I nod.

She opens the door and we step into 1978.

Over the years, the rest of the house had been updated and remodeled more than once, but not this room. This room is a time capsule, exactly as it was the night Janet vanished off the face of the earth forever.

A single bed with a gold bedspread and rust-colored sheets sits in the corner, its covers tossed to the middle and bunched up. A windowsill with a couple of plants on it. Green shag carpet with clothes and shoes strewn about. An open closet with plaid skirts and flared-bottom jeans hanging on a single bar, boots and shoes beneath it spilling out into the room.

A small, narrow built-in desk. A huge plastic camera

like you'd see in a department store display hanging from the ceiling above it, looming large, dominating everything else in the room.

Both her dresses from that weekend—one for the pageant, one for the ball—like everything else, have been left exactly as they were, one draped over the desk chair, the other over the end of the bed.

"She never kept her room perfect," Verna says. "But because of how busy she was that weekend, it's far messier than normal."

A bulletin board on the wall above her desk is filled with photographs, mostly taken by her, and clippings from fashion magazines and fancy photoshoots.

"Family, photography, and fashion," Verna says. "With a little time left over for her boyfriend, friends, and her horse. That's how my girl filled her short life. And fill it she did."

We look around a little while, but are limited in what we can do and not disturb anything.

"It's like I've gone back in time," Dad says. "Like I was just in here yesterday."

Verna nods. "I experience that every morning when I come in here to tell her I love her and every evening when I come in to tell her about my day."

Dad reaches back and takes Verna's hand. "I'm so sorry," he says.

She squeezes his hand, caressing the top of it with her thumb.

"Sorry it happened. Sorry I wasn't able to find out exactly what happened or why or who did it. Sorry I left. So sorry for all of it. Every damn bit of it."

She starts to say something, but Ralphie yells for her

from the den and she excuses herself to go check on him.

Dad shakes his head. "Before Janet was killed, she had a little help—Janet, even Ronnie—now she has no one. To go through what she has . . . and still be able to take care of . . ."

"Batman?" I offer.

"Yeah."

"You two seem pretty close," I say.

He nods. "We really bonded while I was working on the case up here. Nancy was younger than Janet but not by much. She was into horseback riding at the time. I . . . I really . . . I was able to put myself in Verna's place and . . ."

Eventually, Verna returns. "Batman made a Batmess and needed Batmother to make it better."

"You're so good with him," I say.

She smiles and shrugs. "He's all I've got. And it's easy. He's easy to love. Fun to do stuff for. Not everyone gets to live with Batman."

I nod and smile at her and miss Anna, Johanna, and Taylor something fierce.

"We've seen enough," Dad says. "Thanks for letting us take a look."

He turns to leave, but she lifts her hand to stop him. "There's something I need to tell you."

"What is it?" he asks. "Are you okay?"

"I held something back," she says. "I . . . I hid something. I was just tryin' to protect my baby girl, that's all. And I was going to tell you back then—only you, no one else—but just about the time I was ready to, you left."

"Sorry again that I did," he says. "You can tell me now. And you can say anything in front of John."

She nods. "I know that. He's a good man like you. I

179

can tell."

"So what is it?"

"I took two things out of her room before the police arrived," she says. "And I'd do it again. I don't think they have anything to do with . . . what happened to her, and . . . it would have embarrassed her. She is a private person. Shy, in a way."

Dad nods.

She looks over at me.

I also nod, and give her an encouraging expression.

"I took her diary and . . ."

"And?" Dad says.

"She had lingerie laid out on her bed. It was new and sweet but very sexy. Had red hearts and lace and looked like a Valentine. Her last entry in her diary said she was excited and nervous because she was going to give her virginity to Ben that night."

Dad touches her shoulder tenderly.

"I don't think Ben killed my Janet and I don't think her last diary entry or the fact that she had lingerie laid out had anything to do with what happened to her. And it was too private to . . . I couldn't let the world see that. I couldn't."

Dad nods. "We understand," he says. "I'd've done the same thing if it were my daughter."

"Oh, I know only too well what you're willing to do for your daughter."

Dad looks a little embarrassed. "You should see how John is with his."

"You have a daughter?" Verna asks.

"Two," I say.

"Would you do what I did for them?"

I nod. "I would. That and more."

"What I did wasn't the reason the case wasn't solved, was it?" she says.

Dad shakes his head. "I don't think it was."

She looks at me again.

"I don't either," I say. "I really don't."

As they turn to leave, I step over to the closet and look at the clothes.

Turning back toward me, Verna says, "She had such great taste, such a flair and eye for fashion."

I nod. "She really did."

"Had she worn the outfit she wore to the farmhouse party that night before?"

"What outfit?" she says. "Is there a picture of her there that night?"

"I'm sorry, I figured you would've seen it," I say, reaching into my pocket and bringing out the copy Kathy had given me.

"No," she says. "I didn't know there was one. It would be the last picture ever taken of my baby girl."

She takes the photo from me and pulls it close to her to study it.

In only a moment or so, she is shaking her head and frowning. "I can see why you'd think that was her," she says, "but it's not."

"It's not? Are you sure?"

"Looks an awful lot like her," she says.

"The clothes," I say. "The car."

She studies it even more intently.

"Those are clothes like she would wear but they're not her clothes. She didn't have an outfit like that. To be honest, several of her friends tried to look and dress like her. I bet it's one of them. And the car . . . it has a moon roof. Hers didn't."

"So we have no evidence she was even at the party," Dad says.

"I'd say we have pretty strong evidence she wasn't. The person we thought was her, wasn't."

"Who do you think it is?" Dad asks Verna. "Is it Kathy? She's the one who gave us the pictures."

She shakes her head. "Kathy was influenced by Janet. They were very close. But Kathy never tried to copy Janet to that extent, never tried to look like her."

"Who did?" I ask.

"Wasn't a close friend. Really wasn't a friend at all. Sabrina. Sabrina Henry."

Chapter Thirty-seven

As we leave Janet's room and start back down the hallway on our way out, Dad says, "I'm gonna slip into the den and say goodbye to my crime-fighting buddy Batman."

"He'd like that," Verna says. "Sheriff Jack is one of his heroes."

As Dad walks ahead, I slow my pace hoping Verna will do the same.

She does.

"Shame no one is reading all these great books," she says. "Guess we should find them a better home, maybe donate them to the library. If you see any you'd like, please feel free to take them."

"Thank you," I say. "I might just take you up on that."

"I wish you would."

"I need to ask you something," I say. "I'm only asking as it relates to its impact on the original investigation. That's all. Okay?"

"Okay," she says, her voice and expression uncertain.

"Were you and Dad having an affair before he came here to take over the investigation?"

She takes a step back, her eyes widening in alarm, but quickly recovers, takes a breath and regains her composure. "I didn't know him before he came here to try to find out who killed my little girl. Are we that obvious?"

"Especially when you're trying not to be," I say.

"Have you talked to your dad about it yet?"

I shake my head.

"Are you going to?"

I nod. "I plan to."

"Your dad's a vault," she says. "Good luck getting anything out of him. He saved my life. I'm not sure I . . . what I would've done without him. He quickly became my everything back then—he and Ralphie. I thought God had sent him to me in my darkest hour. Not only was he the closest companion I've ever had, but he was going to bring my little girl's killer to justice. But it wasn't long before he vanished just the way Janet had. He was here and then he was gone. No explanation. No warning. Just gone."

I nod as I think about it, but before I can respond, a loud crashing sound comes from the den and I run toward it.

Crossing the kitchen, I can see through the open doorway into the den. Ronnie Lester, a pistol in one hand and a sword in the other, is telling Dad to get on his knees.

"Swore if you ever came into my house again I'd cut your dick off," Ronnie says.

His words are slurred, his movements shaky, his bearing unsteady, but in a glance he doesn't appear to be too inebriated to do what he swore he would.

I slow down a little, not wanting to run in and startle

him, cause him to squeeze the trigger and shoot Dad in the head.

"We lose our little girl, dying of grief, and you come in and start fuckin' my wife," Ronnie says. "GET ON YOUR GODDAMN KNEES. NOW. She was out of her mind with pain and sorrow and you took advantage of her. Didn't find Janet's killer. Too busy raping her mother."

Dad slowly, unsteadily eases down onto his knees and raises his hands.

Drawing my gun, I walk into the room slowly.

Ralphie, in his Batman costume, is sitting in the recliner just a few feet from Ronnie and Dad, watching with what seems like only mild interest.

Raising my gun toward Ronnie, I edge toward them.

Ronnie glances over at me with no reaction and says nothing to me.

In another moment I know why.

I hear the bat cutting through the air in the instant before it connects with the back of my head and I go down, dropping my gun, blacking out for a few seconds.

"RONNIE," Verna shouts as she runs into the room. "Stop this nonsense right now."

"Shut up, whore," he yells at her, spit flying out of his mouth.

Still dazed I reach for my gun, but it's too far away.

I start to crawl toward it, but the young guy holding the bat steps out from behind me and picks it up.

"This is all your fault . . . you faithless whore."

Jamming the pistol into the waistband beneath his beer gut, Ronnie grabs the sword with both hands and raises it, preparing to strike.

But as he begins to bring it down, the large, old,

overweight Dark Knight in the recliner rises, bringing up his cane, and blocks Ronnie's swing.

"Leave Mommy and Sheriff Jack alone," he says.

He then jabs Ronnie hard in the stomach with the end of the cane, and as he doubles over in pain, hits him on the back of the head, sending him to the floor.

Ronnie drops the sword and tries to catch himself as he goes down.

From all fours on the floor, Ronnie turns his head and looks up at Ralphie. He starts to say something, but Ralphie holds his cane out toward him, one hand on the shaft, the other on the large silver Batman head of the handle, which he pulls on just a bit until the metal of the sword inside gleams in the dull light.

Ronnie freezes and Dad quickly reaches beneath him and grabs the pistol from his waistband.

The guy close to me drops my gun on the floor and runs out of the room.

"It's okay now, Batman," Verna says. "You did good. You can sit back down now."

"Batman and Sheriff Jack," Ralphie says as he collapses back into the recliner. "Crime-stopping crusaders."

Dad nods. "Yes we are," he says. "Yes we are."

Chapter Thirty-eight

"**Y**ou want the whole sordid truth?" Dad asks.

"And nothing but."

"It's plenty ugly," he says.

"I can handle it."

We are in Ronnie and Verna's front yard waiting for Glenn to arrive with a deputy to take Ronnie into custody.

Ronnie, his hands cuffed behind him, sits on the front porch crying the way drunks do.

We are standing in the shade of an oak tree far enough away that he can't hear us, close enough to keep an eye on him. I'm holding an icepack to the back of my head.

"Your mom and me . . . we were never a good match," he says.

I nod. Slowly because my head is throbbing.

"We just didn't . . . fit. Her drinkin' didn't help, but even before it got bad . . . we just weren't . . . But we had kids and we did our best to stick it out and do the best job we could raisin' y'all."

Ronnie is blubbering now.

"Being up here, working this case . . . I was up here a lot. Being away from . . . made me realize just how miserable we were. What I did was wrong on so many levels, in so many ways. But . . . I was so susceptible and she was so vulnerable. I felt so bad for her and she was reaching for anything to cling to . . . and I was there. And we . . . We truly and genuinely fell in love. Sure, it was mixed up in her loss and the case and me being the savior and all that shit, but it was real too."

I nod.

"How hard is this for you to hear?" he asks.

I shake my head. "It's not."

"Really. Why's that?"

"I lived it. We all did. Hearing the truth behind it, getting the secrets out in the open is . . . refreshing."

"I've always tried to be a good man," he says. "Always wanted to honor the badge—live the law not just enforce it for others."

"I know that. And you did. You do."

"This was the only time I was unfaithful," he says. "The only time. But . . . it's not like that makes it any better. I just wanted you to know. I . . . I realize how wrong I was, how bad I fucked up. Hurt so many people. Failed to . . . close the case. And . . ." He shakes his head and I can see moisture in his eyes.

"What? And what?"

"You thought Nancy left and never looked back because of Mom's drinking, didn't you?"

Nancy, my older sister and Anna's best friend back in high school, left home the same day she graduated and never came back—except briefly for Mom's funeral last year.

"Not just—more the overall state of our family, but yeah, that was a big part of it."

"It was mostly because of me, because of what I did."

"She knew about—"

"She was so into horses back then. Wanted one so bad. Verna said she could have Cinnamon, Janet's horse. I brought her up here with me one Saturday to let her look at the horse. Maybe even ride it. The truth is . . . it was mostly an excuse to see Verna."

Verna appears at the front door, looks at Ronnie then us, and gives a little wave.

I wave back and she disappears back into the house.

"She was supposed to be keeping an eye on Ralphie . . . We had already let her ride and told her she could have the horse. She was so happy. So . . . I never saw her like that again. I . . . I just wanted a little time alone with Verna. Just wanted to hold her, to get a chance to talk to her, to check on her. While Nancy was watching Ralphie in his room, Verna and I went out to the barn."

He stops talking, blinks against the moisture in his eyes, shakes his head, and frowns.

He looks so old, so frail, so different from the strong, capable man he was when all this happened back then.

"Ralphie got upset about something. Nancy didn't know what to do, how to calm him. Why would she? She should've never been—*I* should have never put her in that position. She came looking for me, came to ask Verna for help. She . . . She walked in on us. Saw . . . her father fucking a woman not her mother in a barn like an animal."

189

In all this time Nancy had never even hinted at anything like this to me.

"She didn't say a word, just stood there in shock, then turned around and walked over and got in my truck. Never spoke another word to me. Not really. She'd answer a direct question if she had to, but . . . that was . . . She refused the horse. Refused to forgive me. I dropped out of the investigation. Stopped coming up here. Ended things with Verna. Did my best to make it work with her—y'all's mother, but it didn't matter. Even staying single all this time, even after the divorce, even after her mother died. Nothing I've ever done has made any difference. My daughter is as dead to me as Verna's is to her."

Chapter Thirty-nine

A deputy arrives.

While Dad goes over to give him a statement, I call Nancy.

"John? Is everything okay?"

I rarely call her. We seldom talk. The last time we spoke was at Mom's funeral. The last time I called her was to tell her Mom had died.

"Are you alone?" I ask. "Can you go somewhere quiet so we can talk?"

"I'm alone in my apartment. What is it?"

Nancy is an artist living in New York. I don't know much about her life beyond that. I don't know where she lives or if she lives alone or even much about her art.

"How are you?" I ask.

"No. Don't do that, John. Don't ask me how I'm doing. You called for a reason. You have something to say. What is it? Is it Dad? Is he . . ."

"It's about you and Dad," I say.

"There is no me and Dad," she says.

"There needs to be."

"What? What the—"

"We're in Marianna reinvestigating the Janet Leigh Lester case," I say. "He told me what happened at the Lester farm."

"Yeah?"

"Why didn't you ever tell me?" I ask.

"I don't know. I . . . just . . . You and he were . . . I'm not sure. You seemed to have the best chance of any of us at a sane life. I didn't want to fuck up your relationship with him."

"It's time to let this go, Nancy," I say.

"Actually, it's long past time for you to tell me what to do, little brother. That's what time it is. I'm hanging up now."

She ends the call.

I wait a few moments, take a few deep breaths, and call her back.

She answers—which is more than I expected.

"Nancy, please don't hang up. Just listen to me."

"Nothing to listen to. Nothing to say. I let go of all that shit years ago. All of it."

"I don't think you did, don't think you have," I say. "I'm not talkin' turning your back on him and home. I'm talkin' about forgiving him and truly letting it go."

"John, he—"

"Was lonely and unhappy and made a mistake. That's it. There's no more to it than that."

"A *mistake*? A *mistake*?"

She ends the call again.

I take a little longer this time, but eventually call her

back.

She doesn't answer. I get her voicemail.

Anna and Nancy had been best friends all through school. If she won't talk to me, maybe she'll talk Anna. I'll try her one more time. If she still doesn't answer, I'll explain everything to Anna and see if she'll give her a call.

I wait a little longer, breathe a little more deeply, and try her again.

She answers.

"Please don't hang up again. Just hear me out. Okay?"

She doesn't say anything.

"At least consider this," I say. "You wouldn't be so upset about this, wouldn't keep hanging up on me, if you had truly let it go and moved on. This is still affecting you. I'm asking you to hear me out, to really forgive him and truly let this go, for you as much as him."

"Just say what you have to say, John. I'm listening. I won't hang up again. No matter how much I may want to."

"I was asking you a question when you hung up. I'm not asking it to upset you or make you angry. You don't even have to give me an answer. Just answer it for yourself. Okay? In all this time . . . in all your relationships . . . are you tellin' me you've never hurt someone, betrayed someone, done someone wrong?"

She lets out a harsh laugh. "I'm usually the one those things are done to, but yeah. I have. Who hasn't? But only because of my fucked-up family, my—"

"If you get to blame it on your family, on your childhood trauma, then so does he. If you're not responsible for your mistakes, how can you make him responsible for his? You're making him responsible for his *and* yours. If he's responsible, you're responsible. If your family's responsible for yours, then his family is responsible for his."

She doesn't say anything.

We are quiet for a long moment.

Ronnie is in the back of the deputy's cruiser. Dad and Verna are talking to the deputy on the porch.

The silence on the other end of the phone goes on so long I think maybe Nancy hung up again.

"You there?"

"Yeah," she says. "I'm here."

I can tell she's crying.

"You okay?"

"Whatta you think? You just told me I'm no better than he is, that . . . I'm . . ."

"He's never been in another relationship," I say. "Not in all this time. He's still punishing himself, still trying to make it up to you. And you won't even talk to him."

"*Fuck.*"

"I know. One other thing. He's not doing well . . . physically. We're waiting on some tests to know exactly what we're dealing with and what the options are, but it looks like it's cancer."

"Goddamn it, John."

"Whatever time he has left—which could still be a lot, we just don't know—would be far better if you paroled him from this prison the two of you have him in."

She doesn't say anything.

I look over at Verna and Dad together.

"He may even still be able to find some sort of happiness," I add.

The deputy leaves. Verna and Dad embrace. And he heads over in my direction.

"He's walking over here," I say. "Should I put him on the phone?"

"Fuck no. I'm not ready."

"Okay."

"Well . . . okay . . . damn it man . . . put him on."

"You sure?"

When Jack Jordan says "Hello?" he has no idea who's on the other end of the line.

"Daddy."

At that one word—at who's saying it and how it's being said—something inside him breaks.

It's Nancy. She hasn't called him Daddy since childhood. Hasn't spoken to him since then either.

Tears sting his eyes and he doesn't even care.

"Daddy . . . I'm . . . sorry . . . I've been such a—"

"You don't have anything to be sorry for," he says. "I'm the one who's sorry. I'm the selfish bastard who ruined your—"

"I forgive you," she says. "I've been . . . I'm sorry. I should've forgiven you years ago. I was just so young and stupid at the time and I guess I never outgrew it. I forgive you. I understand what you did and why. I really do. I've . . . we've all done similar shit."

He cries even harder as he tries to get it under control and speak so she can understand him.

She's crying harder now too.

"I forgive you," she says again. "But I need you to forgive yourself and I need you to forgive me for being such a bitch about it all this time. I've been so wrong. I'm sorry."

"I love you," he manages to get out. "I love you so much, baby."

"I love you, Daddy. I'm gonna come for a visit real soon."

"I'd love that," he says. "I'd love that so much."

While Dad talks to Nancy, I step over to the porch to check on Verna.

"Sorry about all this," she says. "Ronnie's . . . He's been in a bad way for a long time. He's an addict, which means everything is always someone else's fault. He does everything obsessively. Drink. Gamble. The whole world is out to get him. Life is less fair for him than anyone else. He's put our whole family in jeopardy more than once. He's a user. He uses me. Always has. I've covered for him. I've enabled him. I've put up with . . . more than anybody should. He used Janet. Worked her too hard at his store. Took advantage of her goodness. Even used poor Ralphie like a guard dog, had him watching for loan sharks coming to the house, handed him the phone when debt collectors called. He's . . . he's not a nice person anymore. Hasn't been for some time, but I guess I didn't realize just how bad he'd gotten."

"Are you really apologizing for him?" I ask.

"For my part. For enabling his behavior so long. For . . ."

"You're not responsible for him," I say.

"I'm the reason he's still around," she says. "I should have . . . left him years ago."

"It's not too late."

"No, it's not. And it's done. I'm done. I'm done with him."

We are quiet a moment.

"Do you have any . . ." she begins. "Do you want to ask me anything about me and your dad? I'm sorry for what happened, sorry that I let it happen. For what it did to your family. I was just in such a bad way, so . . . utterly lost."

"You're not responsible for anything that happened in my family," I say. "I understand what happened and why it did—for both of you. Dad was so unhappy. He . . ."

When Dad ends the call with Nancy, he walks over to us and reaches out to hand me the phone—or so I think—but when I step toward him to take it, he grabs me and wraps me up in the biggest hug he's given me since I've been an adult.

He's crying and I can feel the moisture from his tears through my shirt.

I hug him back, holding him almost like a parent would a child—regardless of age—and we remain that way for a long moment.

"Thank you, John," he says. "Thank you my amazing son. Thank you so much."

Chapter Forty

We've pulled it together and are back behind Sabrina's mini mansion again, at a table beneath an umbrella on her patio next to her pool.

When we showed up unannounced at her front door, she asked us to walk around the side of the house to the back like before.

By the time we got there she was waiting with lemonade—just like before.

"I don't wish to be . . . rude, but please understand the position I'm in now and call before you come by," she says.

"Absolutely," Dad says. "Sorry about that. We're tracking down a lead we just got and came straight over. It won't take long. But next time we'll call."

"Hopefully, Sheriff, there won't be a next time," she says.

Today, Sabrina looks even more like a nervous, slightly strung out Patsy Ramsey, and I wonder if for her entire life she's always tried to look like someone else.

"Help us out now and maybe there won't," he says.

"I'll do what I can."

I withdraw the picture from my pocket and hand it to her.

She takes it and looks at it.

"Wow. I look amazing. The light, the way I'm spinning, the way my hair is flying out around my head. Who took it?"

"So it *is* you?" I say.

She nods. "Yeah. Why? Who took it?"

"I'm not sure. Someone in the farmhouse taking pictures that night."

"I don't understand," she says. "Am I missing something? I told you I was there for a little while that night."

"Whose car is that behind you?" Dad says.

"I didn't have a car back then. Didn't have much of anything. Used to borrow my parents' car when they'd let me. My aunt, my mother's sister, was in town that weekend. Came to see me in the Valentine's pageant. She bought me the dress for it so I didn't have to wear Goodwill or hand-me-downs. She bought me this outfit too." She lifts up the picture and waves it back and forth. "I think it was the prettiest I've ever felt in my entire life. And she let me borrow her car. For a little while it was the best night of my life."

"Really?" I ask.

She nods. "I felt so . . . I don't know. It was just a good night, you know? I hadn't had a lot of them. I felt so grown up, so with it. Hip and sophisticated. Had my own car. I looked the cat's ass. It was a magic night for me."

"You came to the party, but didn't go inside," I say. "Is that right?"

"Yeah."

"You didn't stay long, did you?"

"No. Not long."

"What'd you do?"

"Talked to Ben Tillman mostly. He was all sad and . . . He'd been stood up. He'd been drinking and was gettin' pretty drunk. He was convinced that Janet had gone to meet another guy instead of come to the party. His ego was hurt. I tried to cheer him up."

"Who did he think she was with?" I ask.

She looks away and seems to think about it. "Kathy's boyfriend maybe or some other guy he thought she had been secretly seeing. An older guy. I'm not sure."

"So you talked to Ben for a while and then he left with you," I say.

She nods. "He was with me that night," she says. "I've told y'all."

"What happened? Where'd you go? What'd you do?"

"Drove around for a little while. Eventually found a quiet spot to park."

"And?"

"And it was a magic night until . . . He wouldn't look at me when . . . while we were . . . *and* then . . . he said her name as he . . . finished."

"Sorry," I say.

"Wasn't the last time that happened."

"Then I'm really, really sorry."

She shrugs. "All's well that ends well. I'm all good now." She turns a little to take in her home. "I've got everything I always wanted."

"Where did you take him after y'all . . . when y'all left the . . ." Dad says.

"Dropped him off at his house—well, down the block from it."

"What time was that?"

Her eyes narrow and get the accessing-memories look again. "I'm really not sure. It was late, but . . ."

"Were you late gettin' to the party?" I ask.

"A little. Not much."

"And you didn't stay long."

"Right."

"How long did you ride around? How long did y'all park for?"

"A while. Couple of hours probably. Why?"

"Because you provide Ben an alibi for a little while but not nearly the whole night."

Chapter Forty-one

We spend the next couple of hours tracking down the witnesses from the farmhouse party the night Janet went missing—including Kathy, Charles, Gary, Ann, Valarie, and others.

Most we see in person. A few we have to talk to via live video—mostly FaceTime, but at least one on Skype.

We show each of them the picture of Sabrina near her aunt's car and ask if that's who they thought was Janet at the party that night.

Without exception the ones who had said they saw Janet that night say yes, this is the person they believed to be her.

"So we now know she wasn't there that night," Dad says.

We have just gotten back into his truck after questioning the last witness on our list.

"Not for sure, but with a relatively high degree of certainty," I say. "Which argues for it being Bundy instead of Ben."

He nods. "Still want to talk to him again."

"Let's do."

Unlike the basement bar Ronnie hangs out in, we find Ben at an actual bar. We just have to drive seventeen miles outside of town to do so.

"Ben wasn't the one who threatened me in my room," Dad says.

"How do you know?"

"That guy didn't smell of booze."

I smile.

We walk over to the bar and take a seat on either side of Ben.

Ben, who is hunched over his drink, looks up briefly, shakes his head slowly, and returns to the previous position.

The female bartender looks to be in her sixties, but could be younger. She has sun-damaged skin, a smoker's wrinkles around her mouth, a missing tooth, and wariness.

"What'll you have?" she says.

"Bud Light," Dad says.

"Diet Coke and grenadine," I say.

"You serve cops in here?" Ben says.

"Cops and criminals alike," she says as she withdraws a bottle of Bud from the cooler beneath her, pops the top, and places it in front of Dad.

"And another one for him," Dad says, nodding toward Ben.

She smiles. It's a good smile. "Oh, I'm sure he's too principled to take a round from a cop."

"Wait just a . . . just a minute there, Sherry Lynn. Not so . . . fast."

He turns to Dad. "Take care of my tab and my drinks for the rest of the night and you can . . . and I . . . will . . . talk to you."

"You'll answer all our questions honestly?" I say.

He turns toward me. "What'd you say, Mr. Diet Coke and grenadine?"

"I bet you have a pretty sporty tab," I say. "You've got to earn it. Answer our questions honestly."

"Deal," he says, nodding. "I have nothing to hide. Hell, I . . . also . . . have . . . nothing."

Dad takes out his credit card and hands it to Sherry Lynn. "You can run it for his tab and drinks tonight when we're done *if* he answers our questions honestly."

She nods, takes the card, turns around, opens her register, puts it in it, and makes a note on a small notepad on the counter beside it.

"You heard the man, Ben," she says. "Cooperate with them or . . . I ain't runnin' it."

"I have nothing to hide," he says. "I . . . have . . . nothin' at all anymore. 'Cept a lawnmower my old man bought me."

"We know you left the party with Sabrina not Janet that night," Dad says.

"Hold up . . . hold up. You're tryin' to . . . trick me. That's not a question. That's a . . . a . . . the other thing."

"A statement," I offer.

"It's just like . . . Junior says," Ben says. "It's a . . . it's a . . . a . . . statement. But not . . . the kind . . . that's like a . . . bill."

"Why didn't you tell me you left with Sabrina?" Dad says. "You had an alibi. You wasted our time and resources. Why?"

204

"Why?" Ben repeats. "Why? I'll . . . I'm just drunk enough to tell you why."

He pauses to take another swig of his drink.

"Because . . ." he continues. "Because . . . while my girl was being . . . being killed . . . I was bangin' some Janet wannabe."

He starts crying.

Dad and I look at Sherry Lynn.

"Oh, just wait," she says. "That's nothin'. Wait 'til he's had some more and really gets to opening up. He can be one maudlin motherfucker."

"I . . . was . . . I was mad," Ben says. "Thought . . . she stood me up. Thought she was . . . teasing me 'cause she said we were gonna . . . you know . . . for the first time that night. And then she . . . she didn't show. She . . . I . . . I was fuckin' Sabrina while she was . . . while Janet was . . . being . . ."

He has carried around so much guilt for so long it's a part of his molecular structure now. The grief from losing her would have been difficult enough, but together with the guilt it's debilitating.

"Who do you think did it?" I ask. "Who do you think killed her?"

He looks from me to Dad then back to me, his face a mask of confusion. "Bundy," he says. "Right? Has to be. He . . . was . . . got her before she . . . She never . . . made it . . . to the . . . party because . . . he . . . I . . . was there when . . ."

"You were where?" Dad asks.

"When he . . . when they . . . fried him. I . . . drove down there. Stayed . . . up all night . . . outside the . . . prison. I . . . was there for . . . her when they . . . juiced his balls and short-circuited his brainpan. Kicked the shit . . . out of some fuckin' . . . protestor of the . . . death penalty. Told him . . . about what that . . . son of a bitch Bundy did . . . to my . . . girl."

He starts crying again.

"We . . . wouldn't . . . we wouldn't have wound up . . . together. Not . . . not for . . . ever. She was . . . she was too good for . . . me. She was . . . magic. So beautiful . . . so sweet . . . so talented. I worshiped the . . . the ground she . . . walked on."

"Some witnesses said you seemed distracted at the ball and that you two may have been fighting," I say.

He shakes his head. "I . . . was . . . nervous . . . and . . . We had . . . we had talked about goin' all the way that . . . weekend. I . . . I was planning to . . . propose after we . . . or . . . before. I couldn't—"

"Hey, hey, Sherry Lynn," an older man at the end of the bar says. "Turn it up. Look at that. Turn it up."

He's pointing toward the TV hanging on the wall behind us. We turn to see what he's referring to, as Sherry Lynn turns up the volume.

It's a local newscast out of Dothan.

". . . is believed to be the remains of Janet Leigh Lester," a young brunette reporter is saying. "Lester went missing on February 12, 1978. Her car, which was covered in blood, was found in a pasture on Highway 71 not far from the I-10 ramp near Marianna. The sheriff leading the original investigation believed serial killer Ted Bundy was responsible for her disappearance. Bundy was known to be in the vicinity the night in question, but the convicted serial killer, responsible for the deaths of some thirty women around the country, maintained his innocence of the crime up until the time of his execution in Florida's electric chair in 1989. . ."

I look over at Dad.

He shakes his head and frowns. "Guess we can let Eglin know to call off the search over there. Hell, I doubt they've even started yet."

"Where is that?" I ask. "What is she standing in front of?"

Behind the reporter there is a statue or monument of some kind, but it's mostly obscured by police cars and crime scene techs.

"I don't recognize it," Sherry Lynn says.

"They found her?" Ben says. "They found my Janet?"

"Looks like it," the older man who first saw it says.

As Glenn Barnes fills the screen to give a statement, my phone vibrates in my pocket. A moment later, Dad's does too.

"Y'all found her?" Anna asks.

"This is the first we're hearing of this," I say.

"Oh. Okay. I'll let you keep watching. Call me later when you can."

"Will do. Love you."

". . . certain at this point, but we have reason to believe there's a good possibility these are the remains of Janet Leigh Lester . . ."

"How was her—how was she discovered after all this time?" Ben says.

". . . I can't get into any specifics," Glenn says. "This is an ongoing investigation, but I'll be giving a press conference just as soon as we have information to share. . ."

Dad is nodding, the phone still pressed to his ear. "I'm on my way," he says.

Disconnecting the call, he stands.

I pat Ben on the back. He's crying even harder now and looks like he's about to lean too far forward and fall out of his chair.

"I need to get over to Verna's," Dad says. "She just saw this like everyone else. Bastard didn't notify her or warn her in any way." Then to Sherry Lynn, "Can you total us up, including Ben's tab?"

"Sure, sugar," she says, still shaking her head as she watches the TV. "Can't believe after all this time they found her. Wonder how?"

"I wonder that too," I say.

"Me too," Dad says, "and I plan to find out."

Chapter Forty-two

When we walk into Verna's house, we find Darlene Weatherly, the short, thick, muscular deputy Glenn had asked to search for similar cases.

She and Verna are in the den alone. Ralphie is in his bedroom and Ronnie is still in custody.

"John," Darlene says, nodding to me as we walk into the room.

"Oh, Jack," Verna says, rushing over to Dad, the two of them embracing. "Can you believe . . . after all this time."

"This is my dad, Jack Jordan," I say to Darlene. "Dad this is Darlene Weatherly, the deputy I mentioned to you who's looking into the similar cases."

Though embracing Verna, Dad nods. "Nice to meet you."

"Can you believe we had to find out about this on TV?" Verna says.

"No, I can't," Dad says. "I was surprised I didn't get a call, but I'm shocked you didn't get a—"

"That's what I'm here for," Darlene says. "I'm very

sorry I didn't get here sooner. Sheriff Barnes said to please convey his apologies. He had no idea the media would be there and report on it so soon. He's very sorry. He said to tell you that he'll be by in person as soon as he can. Before the press got involved, he wanted the opportunity to verify that it was her before getting your hopes up."

"This is not how any of this should've been handled," Dad says.

"Where was she found?" I ask.

She shakes her head. "I'm sorry. I can't say."

Dad says, "It was on TV for everyone to see but you can't tell us."

"Sorry," she says, frowning and shrugging. "I can tell you that John here's the reason we found her."

"What do you mean?" Verna asks, then looks at me. "What does she mean?"

I shrug. "I'm not sure."

"It was him asking us to look for similar cases that led us to her. If I hadn't been looking at old cases, I would've never uncovered the . . . what I needed to . . . in order to find her."

Verna starts to ask her something else, but Darlene holds up her hand.

"I'm real sorry," she says. "I am. But I've already said more than I was supposed to. The sheriff will be over to talk to you as soon as he can. He'll have a lot more information for you and can answer your questions. I'm very sorry for your loss, but I am glad we finally found her for you. I'm gonna go now, but—"

"Tell me this before you do," Verna says. "Is Ronnie getting out of jail tonight?"

"No, ma'am, he's not."

"Can you make sure I'm notified when he does? I don't want to be alone with him. I want someone here with me when he comes home. Preferably the police, who can be here while he packs a few things then escort him out."

Darlene nods. "I'll make sure you're notified, but it won't be tonight—and probably not even tomorrow."

"Thank you. And thanks again for your part in helping find my baby girl."

"You're so welcome. Good night, ma'am."

She turns and starts to leave the room.

"I'll walk you out," I say.

Chapter Forty-three

By walking Darlene out, I not only give Dad and Verna a little time alone together but can see if I can get any more information out of her.

We walk back through the open kitchen and living room, through the photograph-covered foyer, and out into the warm, humid night.

As soon as we're outside she says, "How good are you at keeping shit to yourself?"

"The best. You can tell me anything. It'll stay between us."

"I can't believe that glory-hogging bastard didn't even let y'all know what we had. He's such a fuckin' prick. You know what the extent of the credit you'll get will be? An anonymous tip. That's it. You'll be an anonymous tip. And I won't be shit. It was your idea and my work that found her, but . . . we won't get . . . Look at where I am and what I'm doin' while they're over there at the crime scene I led them to. I'm sick of it."

"Where is it? Where'd you find her?"

"A little park on Caverns Road."

"How?" I say. "How'd you find her?"

"By doin' what your ass asked me to do—looking at every crime that's occurred since she went missing—and a few from a little before."

"I didn't say every crime. I said every homicide and missing person case—anything that had any similarities to—"

"Well . . . good thing I misunderstood you, 'cause . . ."

"How sure are you it's her?"

"As sure as we can be without some sort of DNA confirmation or something like that, but it's her."

"How do you know?"

"Clothes. Jewelry. ID in what was left of her wallet. Only bones left of her, but she was wrapped in some sort of blanket or something and then a nylon or polyurethane material around it. Preserved everything about as good as could be expected without a coffin."

I think about what that means.

"You know I know a lot more about this case than anybody realizes," she says.

"Oh yeah?"

"Doesn't matter. It's just frustrating. I've read and studied it and thought about it for years and . . . nobody ever even asks what I think."

"What do you think?" I ask.

She smiles. "I didn't mean you, but . . . I'll tell you sometime. Anyway, they already got her dental records from her dentist—local guy still in practice, though his son mostly runs it now. They're checking her records against what they found, but it's her."

"Tell me about the park where she was found," I say.

"It's very small. More of a monument garden than park. Local black civic group built it back in 2000. It's called Tree of Peace or the Peace Tree or something like that. I don't know a lot about it, but I think it has something to do with the last spectacle lynching in the country that took place here back during the Great Depression. Maybe some other racial shit. Dozier maybe."

"What made you look there?"

"I got lucky. I looked at some shit and made a guess or two."

"Tell me."

"I'll tell you, but only because I don't trust Glenn and I won't be here much longer. But don't you do anything to hurt me with this. I've applied to work with the highway patrol. Don't fuck that up for me."

"I won't."

"Two crimes and a few odd occurrences happened on the same night back in 2000. We had a hit-and-run victim on the road not far from the garden thing, which was under construction at the time. Thing is . . . it was weird. The victim, a young girl named Naomi about Janet's age, was found on the side of the road. It was bad. You've never seen a body so mangled and . . . looked like she'd been hit by something big, like a semi tractor-trailer, and then dragged for a long ways down the road. It was . . . It's hard to even think about. Thing is, she had some cuts and injuries not consistent with being hit and or dragged by a vehicle. Like she had been stabbed and her throat slit, but . . . ME said it could've been a murder made to look like a hit-and-run or she could've gotten the injuries in some weird way from the vehicle. It's been open all this time.

214

Reading about it this time . . . in the light of what happened to Janet . . . I don't know, I guess I saw it in a new way. I thought about all that blood in her car and then I thought about this other girl being cut and . . . I don't know . . . it just made me wonder. I thought it was a long shot, but I pulled the file to show you and the sheriff and then I saw this other shit that happened near there that same night and . . . I don't know, it just clicked a little."

"What else happened that night?"

"A tractor with a backhoe was stolen and the garden monument was vandalized. Part of the installation is a full-size bronze tree with a noose hanging in it—you know, for all the lynchings. It was dug up and knocked over, but the more I looked at it . . . the more I saw that it wasn't knocked over so much as carefully laid over on its side. It wasn't damaged in any way. All they had to do was get a backhoe and lift the tree and put it right back in the ground. Hell, they went to the same construction site down the road and borrowed the same one that had been stolen to do it. Because of the way it was done—all careful like—I thought maybe it was a distraction, a decoy, from what was really going on. There was another spot in front of the monument that looked like it had been disturbed. They had recently laid sod around the new monument and it looked like it had been moved a little—but only a little. But it was enough to notice. It was like when you dig a hole and put the dirt back in and there's more than enough so it's raised up some. It was like that. But because the tree was the focus and looked like it was what had been vandalized, everybody thought the tractor just disturbed the area. They took pictures of it, notated it, but didn't really investigate it. And I get it. Looked like there was nothing to investigate, but when I looked at the pictures, I could tell the sod had been laid back down too neatly to be explained by a tractor running over it. I figured it was nothing, but thought it was possible it was something. You know, worth taking a look at. So we did. I wasn't sure what to expect but it damn sure wasn't Janet Leigh Lester, I'll tell you that."

"Good work," I say. "Very nice. That's some truly impressive investigating."

"Lot of luck. Just stumbled onto it really."

I shake my head. "Not luck. Damn fine police work. You have any idea how many people would have looked at exactly what you did and never see anything?"

Her face flushes crimson. "Thanks. Thank you. A lot. I . . . I really appreciate it. I need to go. Please don't breathe a word of this to anyone."

"I won't."

"Swear."

I nod. "I won't."

"Then I'll tell you the most troubling part."

"What's that?"

"The sheriff's brother, Brad, worked on that construction site. He . . . I think Glenn is covering up for him. Think that's the real reason you're being shut out."

Chapter Forty-four

The torture and murder of Claude Neal, a twenty-three-year-old farm laborer who lived about nine miles outside of Marianna with his wife, mother, and aunt, has been called the last public spectacle lynching in US history.

Lola Cannady, a twenty-year-old white woman who had grown up near Neal, left her family home on Thursday, October 18, 1934, to walk to a water pump to water the family's hogs, and never came home again.

Neighbors helped the Cannady family search for Lola in the fields behind the family's farm, and early the following morning found her body in the woods under the cover of a couple of logs and pine tree branches. She had been bludgeoned to death with a hammer used to mend fences taken from her family's own field, and it was also later determined that she had been raped.

I'm on the uncomfortable couch in Verna's den reading the rest of the murder book and information about Claude Neal, the disgraceful racial history of Marianna, and the monument and garden commemorating it where Janet's body was discovered. Dad is asleep in Ralphie's recliner beside me.

He insisted on staying here tonight and I didn't feel like I could leave him here alone.

I had gone by the garden earlier in the night to try to talk to Glenn Barnes or get a look at the crime scene, while Dad and Verna dealt with a news crew that showed up at her door, but Glenn was gone and the deputies posted on the perimeter wouldn't let me back where FDLE was continuing to process the scene.

The sheriff at the time of Lola Cannady's death, Flake Chambliss, arrested Neal within two hours of finding Lola's body in a field near her family's farm. According to reports, Claude Neal's aunt and mother were found attempting to clean blood from Neal's clothes, and a piece of cloth appearing to match those clothes was found near Lola's body.

By the next day, area newspapers were printing stories about Neal and racial tensions in town were already beginning to intensify. With only two deputies, Sheriff Chambliss decided his department would be unable to protect Neal from the growing mob wanting to lynch the young man, so he decided to move Neal through a series of different jails.

Transported across state lines to the Escambia County Jail in Brewton, Alabama, and booked under the name John Smith on a vagrancy charge, Neal remained in custody there. Following a coroner's jury back in Marianna determining that Neal raped and murdered Lola Cannady, and that his mother and aunt were feloniously present as accessories, Neal's whereabouts were leaked to the press. A lynch mob from Marianna broke Neal out and carried him back home to a spot in the woods near Peri Landing along the Chattahoochee River.

Neal was tortured and castrated, his genitalia shoved in his mouth and down his throat, was stabbed, burned with hot irons, had his toes and fingers removed, and was hanged before his dead body was tied to a vehicle and dragged to the Cannady property. Outraged that he had not been the one to kill Neal, George Cannady shot his corpse three times in the forehead. Further mutilation of the body ensued by the moonshine-drunk crowd gathered there, which included kids who stabbed the body with sharpened sticks. The mob then began to burn down shacks around the area where black families lived.

Later that night, the mutilated body of Claude Neal was hung up outside the town courthouse. When Sheriff Chambliss discovered it early the next morning, he cut it down and buried it.

A mob of some two thousand people formed outside the courthouse, excited to see the lynching, and demanded that Chambliss dig up the body and hang it back up again when they realized they were too late to see it. When Chambliss refused, they purchased pictures of the corpse for fifty cents each and started rioting. Some two hundred African-Americans were injured. The police were also attacked. Eventually, the National Guard arrived and ended the riots.

But they couldn't end what caused them to begin in the first place. And the fear and hate and mistrust and racism continued to fester just beneath the surface. Always there. Always about to boil over.

Never formally indicted nor arraigned, Claude Neal was believed by many to be innocent. Rumors of other suspects and scenarios swirled around but no investigation was conducted. Governor Sholtz called for a grand jury investigation into the lynching, but in spite of several news articles providing possible leads as to the identities of those involved, the grand jury merely concluded that the lynching was perpetrated by persons unknown.

No further investigations were conducted and the governor absolved Chambliss of any personal responsibility in the matter.

But Marianna's racial tensions and atrocities didn't begin or end with Claude Neal.

By 1930, some four thousand black men had been lynched nationwide, most in the Deep South, and though Alabama and Mississippi had more total lynchings, Florida had the highest per capita rate during the first thirty years of the twentieth century.

Like most cities in the Deep South, systemic racism and brutality are part of Marianna's shameful blood-stained history, but this little town seems to have been a place of heightened savagery and wicked extremes.

Four years after the Civil War ended, Marianna and Jackson County were the center of a low-level guerrilla war conducted by the Ku Klux Klan known as the Jackson County War. Members of the Klan, many of them Confederate army veterans, murdered over one hundred fifty government officials and African-Americans.

Another racial blight on the small town of Marianna is that of the Florida School for Boys, or Dozier School for Boys, the reform school operated by the state of Florida from 1900 to 2011. The school had a reputation for abuse, beatings, rapes, torture, and even murder—all of students by staff. A staff it seems was made up of many Klan members. From 1932 to 1936, twelve young African-American boys died inside Dozier. According to school officials, all twelve died of pneumonia. Over the course of its corrupt history, at least sixty-five young boys died. Many, many more lived cruel little lives of rape and torture, humiliation and degradation.

The garden monument where Janet's remains were discovered is meant to be a reminder of all of this plus a place of peace and hope for a better, more civil future.

An image of Janet appears in my mind, unbidden, and sparks a series of thoughts that lead to a series of questions.

I pull out Janet's picture and look at it again.

It's so subtle, but it's there.

I push myself up off the couch and walk out into the living room.

As I begin to head down the hall toward Verna's room, I see a large dark figure near the front door.

Chapter Forty-five

The figure doesn't move.

His back is to me.

Placing my hand on the weapon holstered at my right side, I slowly move toward him.

As I get closer, I see that it's Ralphie's Iron Man costume standing near the front door.

The suit looks amazingly like the one from the movie—though much larger. Ralphie isn't in it. It's just the suit, and even in the dimness of the foyer it looks like metal.

Walking down the hall toward Verna's room, I stop at Ralphie's room to check on him.

As I stand there looking at him, he opens his eyes. "Everything okay?"

I nod.

"Iron Man still watching the front door?" he asks.

"He is."

"Ralphie you have some amazing costumes."

"Not Ralphie. Tony Stark."

"Sorry."

"Let me know if there's any trouble. Sheriff Jack

said there might be."

"I'm staying on the couch, buddy," I say. "I'll keep watch tonight. You just get some sleep."

"You sure?" he asks.

"Absolutely."

"Be very vigilant," he says. "Ronnie is a very bad villain."

"I will."

I continue to the last door at the end and tap on it. The light is on so I'm hoping she's awake.

"Verna?" I say. "It's John. Are you awake?"

She opens the door, a robe wrapped around her. "What is it? Is everything okay? Where's Jack?"

"Yes. Everything's fine. Dad's asleep. I've just been studying the case some more and have a couple of questions for you. They can wait 'til morning—I just didn't want to."

"No, of course," she says. "I appreciate you working on it. Please come in."

She leads me over to a small sitting area in the far corner of her room and we sit in the two high back chairs there.

Between the chairs on a small round table is a stack of newspapers and magazines.

"We used to read books here," she says. "Now I'm the only one who uses it—and just for short reading."

I nod and think again about how everything in her life changed on that February night so long ago.

"Did you uncover something else in the file?" she says. "I still can't believe they found her. I know they never would have if it weren't for you and Jack. Thanks so much for all you're doing. Thanks for helping him, for taking care of him. He's very lucky to have you."

"Thank you," I say. "I'm sorry you two didn't have more . . . of each other over all these years."

"You are?" she asks in surprise.

I nod.

"It surprises me you'd feel that way," she says. "Your mom and—"

"I wish both of them could have had more happiness over the years," I say. "Wasn't something they were going to have together."

Tears glisten in her eyes and she pats my hand. "So much sadness in this world. So much . . . suffering."

We are silent for a moment.

"Anyway. Thank you," she says. "What questions did you have?"

"It's about Janet's biological father," I say. "There's no mention of him in the book."

"The book?"

"The file."

"Oh. Well . . . he was never part of Janet's life. He didn't even live here at the time. Ronnie's the only father the kids have ever known."

"But we should at least talk to him," I say.

She shakes her head and frowns. "He actually passed away a few years back," she says. "Outlived his daughter, but . . . still managed to die relatively early. He had a hard life. But there's no way—absolutely no way he could kill his child. Some people aren't capable of that. Your dad couldn't harm you. You couldn't harm your daughters. Janet's dad and I couldn't harm her. Not ever. No way."

I nod. She's right. I can tell what she's saying is true. But after what Ralphie said and the way Ronnie acted earlier in the day I want to ask her if she believes the same to be true of stepparents.

"Most parents would do anything for their children. Anything at all. I've always been that way. So was Janet's father."

"But he wasn't in her life in any way, was he? He . . . I noticed his name is not even on the birth certificate."

"That's what he did for her," she says. "He stayed away."

"Because he was black?" I ask.

Her eyes widen. "How did you . . ."

"I was reading about all the racial issues this little town has had," I say. "I was thinking about that when I started wondering about why Janet's father wasn't in the file and . . . then I looked at her picture again. The hint of caramel in her skin, certain features, her stunning beauty. I just . . . most everything I do in this kind of work involves a mental, psychological, or spiritual leap."

"It happened when we were in school," she says. "In a very different time. We had genuine attraction and affection for each other, but knew we could never . . . that nothing could ever come of . . . and then I got pregnant. As far as I know, he never knew. I never told him. We stopped seeing each other and I dropped out of school, went to stay with my aunt in Montgomery to have her. He had nothing to do with it. I asked your dad not to investigate him, told him he was dead back then."

I nod.

"He had nothing to do with it," she says. "He was one of the most gentle and loving men I've ever known. There's something about your and your dad's spirit that reminds me of him. Probably why I clung to your dad when it happened."

"Even if he didn't kill her—"

"He didn't," she says.

"Remember what I said about connections? About making leaps?"

"Yeah?"

"You say that Janet's father had nothing to do with her death, but think about where her body was discovered. Think about the racial history of this place and the fact that she was a biracial child and where someone buried her."

Her eyes widen.

"Her father may not have killed her," I say, "but that doesn't mean her death has nothing to do with him."

Chapter Forty-six

"Look, you know how these things work," Glenn Barnes is saying. "They move fast. Don't always have time to call everyone or . . . worry about everybody's feelings."

Dad and I are in his office. It's early the next morning.

"Y'all said y'all didn't care about who gets credit," he says. "I thought y'all meant it."

"We did," Dad says. "It's not about credit. You won't find us talking to the media or trying to take any credit for anything. That's not what we're talking about."

"Then what?"

"Just to be involved," Dad says. "To have the chance to collaborate, to share information. We're uncovering quite a bit. Feel like we're getting close and—"

"You're supposed to be sharing everything you come up with," Glenn says. "But you know how it is. It'd be the same way if I was in your county conducting a private investigation. It's a one-way street. You're supposed to turn over anything you find to me, but I don't have to report to you."

"I know," Dad says. "But under the circumstances . . . I just thought you might . . ."

"Look, I've got enormous respect for both of you. I do. And I appreciate what you're trying to do. I do. But even if I wanted to . . . the DA is . . . I'll be honest with you. When y'all showed up here saying you were going to ask a few questions, see if you missed anything the first time, I didn't think anything would come of it. Things are different now. Now this is an active investigation again. Like it hasn't been in thirty some years. We found her. After all this time. We found her. We may actually be able to close this thing."

"You'd have a better chance of doing it with our help," I say.

"You found her," Dad says. "But how?"

"I can't get into it. I'm sorry. I really am."

"And finding her now, when you did, has nothing to do with what John and I have been doing? It's just a coincidence that you found her remains after thirty-eight years while we're here conducting an investigation?"

"See, Sheriff," Glenn says, "that sounds like you're looking for credit again."

"I'm not looking for any goddamn credit," Dad says, his voice rising, though still weak and not very loud. "I want to close this case."

"You want it closed?" Glenn says. "*Or you want to close it?* Because you can't issue any subpoenas, you can't serve any search warrants, you can't make any arrests. So how exactly would you close it?"

"I just want it done and done right."

"Oh, the way you did it the first time? Right like that? Are you—*you* of all people—questioning my abilities? Are you saying you lack confidence in my department?"

"That's not what I'm saying."

"You know how much this means to him," I say. "You know how personally invested he is in finding Janet's killer."

"Thought he already had," Glenn says. "Thought Bundy did it."

"Maybe he did," Dad says.

"Oh yeah? Then how the hell did he move the body eleven years after he died in the arms of old sparky's warm embrace?"

Chapter Forty-seven

"Come again?" Dad says.

"You heard me. Her remains were moved over a decade after Bundy was executed. The Tree of Peace monument was built in 2000. She wasn't there when they started. The ground where we found her remains had been dug up and bulldozed and leveled and sodded—as the garden was being built. She wasn't there. Someone moved her and buried her there just as they were completing work on the monument."

"Where was she moved from?" I ask.

"We don't know. And I'm not going to get into all the details of this whole thing with y'all. I just wanted you to know that your Bundy theory was bullshit."

Dad doesn't say anything, just sits there stunned, speechless, saddened. Eventually, he frowns, shakes his head, and looks down.

"Sorry to be so . . . but . . . I'm just being truthful," Glenn says. "And if you really care about justice for Janet, you'll be happy I am, because I'm gonna solve this thing."

"We still gonna be able to meet with your brother

Brad?" I ask.

He shakes his head. "Don't see any point in it now. But don't you worry, I'm reinterviewing everyone—including him."

"Are you saying he won't talk to us?"

He shakes his head and sighs. "I've been about as patient and accommodating as I can be. But you guys just don't stop pushing, do you? What I'm sayin' is you need to go back and work on solving cases in Gulf County. We've got Jackson County covered."

I start to say something but stop.

I want to ask him if it's true his brother worked on the garden installation and actually operated the backhoe it now looks like was used to bury Janet's remains there, but know it will only serve to cause problems for Darlene Weatherly.

"I've got a man in custody," Glenn says. "A man who in every way that matters was the father of the victim, and he says that instead of working the case like you should have back then you were carrying on with his wife, the mother of the victim out of her mind with grief and still in shock. Is that true?"

Dad doesn't respond, just holds Glenn's gaze.

"That's not just negligence," he says. "That's gross misconduct. You know what . . . I wasn't going to say anything else about the case, but I've changed my mind. I'll tell you a little something else about the case you botched back then. Guess who worked on both the golf course project where the backhoe was stolen from and the Peace Tree project where Janet was buried? Hell, he's still the yard man there to this day. That's right. Janet's boyfriend, the most obvious suspect. Oh, and the son of the man who asked

231

you to come in here and take over the case. What was it, only on the condition that you set up someone else? Hell, who better than fuckin' Ted Bundy for that? Ted Bundy. You might as well have said the goddamn boogeyman did it."

"**W**hy move the body?" I ask.

Dad doesn't respond. He's still despondent, defeated, disheartened.

"I was feeling so hopeful this morning," Dad says. "Was thinking I might just beat back the cancer for a while and maybe even find a little happiness with Verna for whatever time we have left, but . . ."

"Come on. Help me. We've got to figure this out before Barnes does irreparable harm to it."

"I'm the one who did irreparable harm to it. Me. Not him. Not anyone else. Just me."

"We can still do this," I say. "We're close. Think about how much we've learned."

He shakes his head. "Take me back to the hotel. I'm tired. Need to rest."

"Wouldn't you rather go to Verna's?"

He shakes his head again. "I'm . . . All I do is make her difficult life all that more difficult. Take me to the hotel now."

"Okay," I say, and start the truck.

"Sorry," he says. "I'm just . . . I don't feel very . . . Sorry."

While Dad rests, I drive out Caverns Road to try to take a look at the Tree of Peace memorial garden again.

On the way, I call Daniel Davis.

"Hey man. How's it going? How's Sam today."

"Little improvements every day," he says.

"How about you? How are you holdin' up?"

"Enjoyed y'all's visit," he says. "Always does me good."

"We'll be back soon. Promise."

"Thanks."

"Got a quick question for you."

"Shoot."

"Do you or Sam have any friends in the FDLE lab who would talk to me?"

"About the Bundy thing?"

"The victim's remains were found, and now the sheriff has shut us out. I just have a couple of questions about what was found, very unofficially."

"I know just the person," he says. "I'll call her and get back to you."

"Thanks man. I really appreciate it."

Chapter Forty-eight

The Tree of Peace memorial is both majestic and disturbing. At its center is a life-size bronze tree similar to the one in front of the court house that Claude Neal's mutilated corpse hung from. On one side of the tree a series of nooses hang from the branches, on the other, black and white children climb the branches and push each other in a rope swing that looks like a larger version of one of the nooses.

It's as if in this Eden the tree of life and the tree of the knowledge of good and evil are now one tree.

Around the tree are stone steps with inspirational quotes and markers with historical information on them.

Well-watered and cared for by Ben Tillman, the garden is verdant, both green and flowering.

Though it's still taped off with crime scene tape, the FDLE crime scene techs are gone. Only a single deputy remains to guard the perimeter.

When I see that it's Darlene Weatherly, I pull up, park, and get out.

"You do a little of everything, don't you?" I say.

"Just the shit detail," she says, then her voice changes, taking on an upbeat sarcastic tone. "'It's something nobody wants to do—I know, let's give it to the lesbian. Maybe we can get her to quit.' But I won't."

"Good for you," I say. "And I'm sorry it's that way."

"Won't be forever," she says.

I nod. "Nothing is. Some things just feel like they are."

"You ain't just whistling Dixie there," she says.

My phone vibrates in my pocket and I take it out. It's a Tallahassee number and I figure it's someone from FDLE calling me back.

"Sorry," I say. "I need to take this."

"No problem. I'm not going anywhere."

I step a few feet away. "Hello."

"This John Jordan?"

"Yes."

"This is—this is a friend of Sam and Daniel's."

"Thanks so much for calling me."

"I didn't. I didn't call. We never spoke. I don't know what you're talking about."

"I understand."

"I'd do anything for Sam, but this is . . ."

"I understand and I really appreciate it."

"Rather than you askin' me questions, I'm just gonna tell you all we know—because it isn't much and won't take but a second."

"Okay. Thanks."

"The remains were wrapped in a pretty standard blanket from that era. Nothing out of the ordinary about it. But it's consistent with the 1978 burial date. So is the tent material that is covering it."

"So the nylon material around the blanket is from a tent?"

"Yes. Again, a common tent material from the time. Everything is consistent with a late-seventies burial. But we know the remains were dug up and moved in 2000—and not only because they couldn't've have been where they were found before 2000 but because there are two different types of soil. The soil from the garden where the remains were found is sandy. It was brought in when they were building the memorial park. But based on other soil traces we found, the body was originally buried in soil found in most pastures and yards around the Jackson County area. I can't tell you why her remains were moved, only that they were—all together with all her belongings inside the tent wrap just like they had been buried."

"Thank you," I say.

"For what?" she says. "I didn't tell you anything. We didn't even talk."

She disconnects the call and I step back over to where Darlene is guarding the perimeter.

"Sounds like you may have been getting classified information on an official police investigation," she says.

"You gonna tell Glenn?"

"Might feel compelled to if he actually listened to me or had me working on the case, or . . ."

"Or what?"

"You weren't the only one who didn't treat me like a fuckin' leper."

I shake my head. "Sorry that's the case, but I'm glad you won't be turning me in."

"Who were you talkin' to?" she says.

"Not who I really need to," I say.

"Who's that?"

"The ME or someone in his office. It's funny, I talk to him all the time about my cases in Gulf County, but he won't talk to me at all about a Jackson County case."

The Medical Examiner's Office for the 14th District covers Bay, Gulf, Holmes, Calhoun, Washington, and Jackson counties, and though we all share the same ME, he won't share information about our cases with investigators from other counties—investigators he routinely communicates with otherwise.

"My only hope," I continue, "was an investigator in the office who's a friend, but she's on vacation this week."

Darlene nods and purses her lips, a twinkle in her eyes.

"What is it?" I ask.

"If only you knew someone who had given one of the young ladies in their office the night of her life."

"If only," I say.

"If only you knew someone who had just gotten a job with the highway patrol and didn't give a fuck."

"If only," I say again.

"It'll probably mean I'll have to provide another night of toe-curling ecstasy, but . . . I could be convinced to take one for the team."

"Congratulations on getting the job. Happy for you. If it doesn't work out, there's always a place for a good cop like you in Gulf County."

"What's the lesbian scene like over there?"

"Sort of quiet," I say. "You'd be just the thing to liven it up."

A big, broad grin spreads across her face. "Give me just a minute to make a call," she says, pulling her phone out. Punching in a number, she says, "Hey baby girl, how you been?" as she steps away, back toward the Peace Tree memorial.

As she talks to Baby Girl, I look at the memorial some more and think about the case, attempting to put the pieces together in some coherent order. I think about the ignorance and hatred and fear and small-minded racism that led to such a beautiful memorial, but also about the hope for change and understanding, compassion and equality it also represents.

Does Janet's father being black have something to do with her death? Was it Bundy and someone else who buried her and moved her remains for some reason?

As I gaze at the powerful work of art, I see an older black man doing the same down the way.

I walk over to him.

He's tall and thin and very light skinned. His narrow frame is bent a little, and he's dressed more formally than most people you encounter in the rural, casual South. In his left hand he holds a small bouquet of flowers.

"Incredible, isn't it?"

"Thank you," he says.

"You—"

"Designed it. Yeah."

"You are gifted. It's . . . a stunning work of art."

"Thank you."

He doesn't look at me, just continues staring at his work.

There is something about him, some familiarity . . . and I realize who he reminds me of. Given the resemblance to Janet and the fact that he's here with flowers, I can't help but wonder if he's her biological father.

"You from here?" I ask.

He nods.

"I'm John Jordan, by the way," I say, extending my hand.

"Langston," he says.

His hand is bony, the skin rough and dry.

"You're a true artist, Langston."

"Thank you."

"What brings you back out here today?" I say.

He shrugs. "Just wanted to see . . . it."

"Are the flowers for Janet Lester?"

He looks at them as if he wasn't aware they were there.

"Just figured it's what people were doing. Leaving flowers. But haven't seen any others."

"Yours can be the first," I say. "I'm sure others will bring some to join yours."

He nods, then slowly bends down and places the flowers on the ground in front of the crime scene tape.

"Do you have a daughter?" I ask. "I see some family resemblance."

He shakes his head. "Got no daughter. I've got to go. Excuse me."

"Wait. I just—"

But he is gone, walking away faster than I would have thought him capable, climbing into his car, and speeding away.

I'm writing down his plate number when Darlene returns with a self-satisfied smile on her face.

"Well?" I ask. "What'd she say?"

"I have a date Friday night."

"That's great, but not what I meant."

She laughs. "Oh. Well, it's all preliminary, and they've called in a forensic anthropologist, but she says she doubts they'll find much more than what they have now. There's just not much remains that old can tell you. What they do know is that it is her. Dental records confirmed her identity. There's not much else . . . except there are no broken bones or signs of blunt force trauma that left the skull fractured or anything. Based on the blood in the vehicle and the presence of arterial spray, they believe she was stabbed to death, killed in her car. And there are nicks and scrapes on some of her bones that support that theory. He stabbed her so violently, he scraped and scratched and cut bone. It was a vicious attack."

Chapter Forty-nine

Jack Jordan can tell someone is in the room with him, but he gives no indication. He just goes about his normal routine and appears to collapse into bed the way he had the last time someone was in the room with him.

Only this time, he gets in a slightly different position, and he quietly and quickly pulls his borrowed gun out.

So this time when the man climbs on top of him and attempts to pin him down, Jack shoves the barrel of the revolver into the soft skin beneath the man's chin and thumbs back the hammer.

"Drop it," Jack says.

The man doesn't move.

"Drop it now or a round is about to travel over nine hundred miles an hour through your mouth and sinus cavity and into your brain."

The man drops the weapon he's holding onto the bed.

"Now lace your fingers behind your head."

The room is dim but from what Jack can make out, the man does as he's told.

"Now very, very slowly, without breaking contact with the barrel of my gun, stand up at the same time I do. But don't let your chin lose contact with the barrel or I'm just gonna start shooting and call housekeeping to sponge you up."

Slowly, awkwardly, the two men push up from the bed to a standing position.

"Keep your hands laced behind your head but turn around. As you do, I'm gonna keep the barrel pressed to you, coming around the side of your neck to the back of your head. Try anything and I'll empty the entire cylinder into your neck, face, and head. Maybe you don't care if I do. You clearly don't value your sorry life coming into my room like this. But think about your poor mama. 'Cause I promise she won't be able to identify you."

"I'm doin' everything you say just like you're sayin' it. Don't shoot."

He then slowly turns around, actually leaning his neck into the barrel as he does so as not to lose contact with it.

When he's completely around, Jack quickly cuffs the man.

Then grabbing him by the cuffs while keeping the gun barrel at the base of his neck, he pushes him across the room and into the chair beside the small table in front of the window.

With the man in the chair, Jack steps back and turns on the light switch by the door.

As if a cat burglar, the man is wearing all black with black gloves and a black ski mask.

"It's more'n two months to Halloween," Jack says. "What the hell were you thinkin'?"

242

"Clearly I wasn't," the man says.

Jack steps back over to him and pulls off his mask.

The man is middle-aged, younger than Jack but too old to be doing shit like this.

Though he doesn't recognize the man, there is something faintly familiar about him, like a family resemblance to someone he's seen recently.

"Who the hell are you?" Jack says.

The man shakes his head.

Jack nods, the puts the barrel of his revolver into the man's forehead. "This may tickle, but don't move. You so much as twitch, the dingy hotel wall behind you's gonna know what's on your mind."

Jack then reaches around to the man's back pocket and wriggles out his wallet.

"Brad Barnes. I knew you resembled someone I'd seen in the last few days. You're the sheriff's older brother, aren't you? It's sad to say and it ain't sayin' much, but looks like he got the looks *and* the brains in the family—what little there were. Your brother know you're here?"

Brad shakes his head. "Told me to stay away from y'all. Hell, told me to stay away from town for a little while."

"Turns out not to have been such bad advice." Jack stops suddenly as if something has just occurred to him, turns and looks at the weapon the man dropped on the bed. "Did you bring my gun back?"

The man nods and Jack retrieves his gun from the bed. After admiring it appreciatively for a moment, he sticks it in the holster on his hip and sings very badly and off key, "Reunited and it feels so good."

"I was just bringing it back to you," Brad says. "Felt

bad for taking it before."

"Let's say for the sake of argument you weren't," Jack says. "What's another reason you might break into my room and mount me like I's your prom date?"

The man shrugs.

Jack steps back over to Brad and places the barrel of the revolver between his eyes. "Let's say that I'm dying of cancer. Let's say I've got nothin' to lose. Let's say you already broke into my room once and there's a police report showing it. Let's say I could punch your ticket right now and call FDLE and tell them what happened and that your brother knew it and is trying to cover up for you. Let's say that though you dealt this play, I hold all the cards. Let's say for all those reasons you play along and answer all my questions truthfully—as truthfully as if your life depends on it. Why did you break into my room and—"

"To scare you. Just to scare you and . . . to get you to . . . drop all this and . . ."

"You coulda just asked. Hell, if I'd've known how bad you wanted me to leave I'd've left days ago. Communication is the key, Brad. How can we know what you want if you don't tell us?"

Brad looks confused as if he's not quite sure he's being fucked with.

Jack pulls the gun back but keeps it pointed at Brad as he sits on the edge of the bed. "Did you kill her, Brad? That why you want me gone so bad?"

"No. Wait. Who?"

"Janet."

"Janet Lester? No. No way. I didn't have anything to do with that. I thought she was . . . I had a crush on her back in the day, but never even told her. Was thinking about it, but then she died. I had nothin' to do with that. Absolutely nothin'."

"Then who?"

"Who what?"

"If you didn't kill Janet, who did you kill?"

"No one. No one on purpose. Maybe no one at all."

"The Jane Doe hit-and-run," Jack says. "You the one that ran over her?"

"I don't know. Maybe. It was my . . . I was on some pretty bad shit back then. But . . . I don't know for sure. And didn't want to find out it was me. That's it. That's why I wanted y'all to stop lookin' into it. Glenn said he'd take care of it, but . . . I just wanted to make sure."

"Why do you think you might have done it?" Jack asks.

"I'm clean now. I am."

"Well it sure as hell ain't helping you think any clearer."

"But then, I was on some really bad shit. I's all over the place. Glenn was a deputy, then an investigator. Got me out of more than a few jams. I'd'a been in jail if it wasn't for him."

"Why do you think you may have been the one who hit her?" Jack says again.

"It was my backhoe. I had my own heavy equipment company. This was just before I lost it. I . . . I was buying drugs rather than making the payments on my equipment. I was doing work for different contractors in the area. Worked on the golf course, the high school, and the Peace Tree thing. A few times I'd wake up on my tractor in the middle of the night not knowing what was going on. Everybody thought my backhoe had been stolen from the golf course that night, but . . . what if my fucked-up ass just thought I was at work? Hard to see a car or even a truck doing what was done to that poor girl. But a tractor . . . She was a transient. What if she was sleepin' in the garden and I . . ."

Chapter Fifty

Janet was so excited, felt so alive.

Her body hummed with electricity and energy and life.

Could there be a better weekend? Ever?

It was the perfect time for her and Ben to make love, for them to give themselves to each other utterly and completely, for the Valentine king and queen to consummate their relationship, unite their two kingdoms. Totally time.

Any doubt and uncertainty she'd had earlier at the dance was now gone.

Whatever had caused him to act distracted or disinterested or whatever it was had nothing to do with her. And it wasn't another girl. She could tell. Whatever it was and whatever caused it passed, it was gone as suddenly as it came, and he was back to his normal sweet self. Thoughtful. Attentive. Affectionate. Sweet as strawberry pie—her favorite.

She was excited, but she was nervous too.

She knew just the thing to help with that. And, as fate would have it, it was on the way.

Fate. Was it fate that she won the pageant and they won king and queen at the ball? Was it fate that she and Ben would make love later? Was it fate that they were together? Were they fated to be together forever, high school sweethearts who would one day celebrate their fiftieth wedding anniversary together?

What was her fate? How much say did she have in it? Were we as free as we seemed or was freedom a total illusion?

She decided she was glad she didn't know her fate, happy to remain blissfully ignorant—because she couldn't be any happier, any more blissful. If things were going to work out—her photography and fashion, her relationship with Ben—it couldn't make her any happier than she already was, and if they weren't . . . it would ruin a perfectly perfect weekend.

As she saw the Gulf Station up ahead, looming and lit up in the dark night, she wondered if in addition to getting a little liquid courage for her she should get some condoms—just in case Ben forgot.

It's not liquid courage, she thought. *I don't need courage. It's liquid relaxer. I just want to relax and enjoy every second of it so it can be perfect like everything else this weekend.*

Should she leave the condoms up to Ben? Should she take that chance? Where would she even get some? She was gonna have a hard enough time asking Little Larry for liquor. No way she could ask him if he sold condoms too.

Wonder if the men's bathroom in the back has a machine?

Was she really going to go into a dirty ol' gas station bathroom to buy condoms?

No. No I'm not.

Then what?

Kathy will have some.

But borrowing them from her would mean she would know, and she wasn't sure she wanted that. Sometimes Kathy was so supportive, so . . . just what a best friend should be, but . . . other times she seemed jealous, seemed like she might . . . actually want to . . . Nah, not Kathy.

Chapter Fifty-one

Before I left the memorial, Darlene's shift ended and her replacement showed up and she decided to come with me.

We are driving down to Chipola Ford to talk to Little Larry Daughtry, the kid who sold Janet a bottle of Dewar's and gassed up Ted Bundy's car the night she disappeared. My phone rings.

It's Dad.

"Got my gun back," he says.

Sounds like that's not all he got back. His voice is stronger than it's been in days.

"How'd you do that?"

He tells me.

"Impressive," I say. "You still got it."

"Not quite ready for the rocking chair *or* the grave-yard just yet."

"No doubt. So what'd he say?"

He tells me, and I think about it.

Before he's finished, Darlene looks up from her phone and says, "Ronnie Lester was just released."

I interrupt Dad and tell him.

"I'm already on my way over to Verna's. Just a couple of minutes away."

"If he shows up and starts acting stupid call the police," I say. "He's not worth the paperwork."

"It won't be a problem."

My phone lets me know I'm getting another call. I pull it back from my ear to look at the screen.

"I'm getting a call from Anna," I say. "I'll come by Verna's a little later."

"Take your time. I'm pulling up now. Everything will be five by five over here."

I click over to take Anna's call. "Hey beautiful. How's my girl?"

"Just heard back from one of my Classification contacts in Central Office," she says. "Clyde Wolf was released from Marion CI yesterday. State of Florida bought him a bus ticket back to Marianna. He arrived this morning."

Little Larry Daughtry is anything but.

A huge man in every way, he is some six feet six inches tall with an enormous low-hanging gut, as if his chest and stomach had both slid down to just above his waist.

"You look like a Mustang driver," he says. "I've got some sweet incentives I can offer you right now. Get you the best deal anywhere."

"As much as I'd love a new Mustang, I'm just here to ask you a few questions. I'm John Jordan. We spoke on the phone."

"Oh, yeah. How are you?"

He shakes my hand and seems genuinely happy to

see me—which is probably how he acts with everyone whether he really is or not.

"I'm good. I really appreciate you taking the time to talk to me."

"Happy to do it. It's so cool you're helping your dad with this. I sure hope y'all can finally figure it out and . . . I saw y'all found her body. That's . . . I mean after all this time. It's just . . . amazing."

I nod. Little Larry seems the type to keep talking with very little prompting, so I just wait.

"I've been thinking about that night ever since we spoke on the phone," he says. "'Course I've thought about that night a lot over the years. Still can't believe I was that close to Ted Bundy. Dude was a little wired but sure as hell didn't seem like what he really was. You know?"

I nod.

"I don't know. I was just a kid, but I wish I'd've known it was him or . . . Wish I could've done something to save Janet. She was a cool girl. Nice. Sweet. Pretty."

"Were they there at the same time?" I ask.

His expression makes him look like a kid in school who has just been asked a question he should know the answer to but doesn't.

"I'm . . . just not sure. They could've been. If they weren't, it was close. They were there within minutes of each other if not at the same time. Neither of them were there long. Didn't take any time to fill up his little car. And she was only there long enough to buy a bottle from me and let me congratulate her and hug her neck."

"Congratulate her for winning Miss Valentine?"

He nods. "Yeah. And Sweethearts' Ball queen. She was . . . You know she was . . . she was excited, I could tell that. Think she was headed to—well, I know she was supposed to be headed to that party, so she was excited about that, I guess. So full of life. But more than anything, what she was, was gracious. She was so genuinely touched that I congratulated her and wanted a hug. It's just the type of person she was. Man, I wish I could've saved her."

"Do you remember anything else at all? Can you picture them leaving the parking lot? Was he following her? Was he still there when she left? Just pulling in? Did he leave before her?"

He squints to think about it, seeming to concentrate as hard as he can.

"Let me see." He closes his eyes. "She was in that red Monarch . . . on her way to the party. I watched her the whole time she was at the station. Always had a bit of a thing for her, you know? She pulled up to the road. Sat there for a moment, though there was no traffic. Not at that time of night on a Sunday. And . . . wait. Wait just a minute. She . . . she . . . Why didn't I realize that before?"

"What's that?"

"She went the wrong way."

"What do you mean?"

"She went the wrong way. She was supposed to be going to that party, right?"

"Yeah?"

"Well she turned and headed the opposite direction from it. She went the wrong way."

Chapter Fifty-two

Little Larry had given me the final piece of the puzzle, the last bit of missing information I needed.

The slowly developing image is now visible, is emerging in vivid, tragic color.

What really happened to Janet the night of her disappearance now unfurls like a flag inside my head, and all I can do is watch it.

As if present to watch it happen, I see what Janet did, the choices and decisions she made, the action she'd taken that had led to her death. It plays in the movie theater of my mind.

"What is it?" Darlene asks. "What're you . . . thinking? Did he say something that made you—"

I nod.

"*What?*"

"I always thought Janet had either been picked up or followed by someone at the party or intercepted on her way to it—either at the gas station or somewhere on Highway 71 near where her car was found."

"We all did."

"But now we know she went the opposite direction of the party."

"Yeah? Oh shit. You know who did it, don't you?"

"I think so. I could be wrong but . . . I think so."

"Well let's hear it. Run it past me and I'll try to poke holes in it."

"Let's start with . . . she never made it to the party. We're now pretty certain about that. And let's say for the moment that Ted Bundy didn't do it."

"Okay."

"Two questions. Why did she turn in the opposite direction from the party and where did she go?"

"Was she meeting someone else? Brad maybe."

"She bought the bottle to take to the party. She was headed there."

"Then what?"

"She forgot something," I say.

"What?"

"She wrote in her diary she planned to sleep with Ben that night for the first time. I think that's why she stopped by to get the liquor. But that's not all she purchased for the occasion. She bought a special negligee to wear when she and Kathy went shopping the week before in Dothan. But sneaking out of the dark house quickly and quietly she forgot it. Her mom said it was still laid out on her bed the next morning."

"So she never got it," Darlene says.

"Right."

"So she was intercepted—only going away from the party and not toward it. She never made it back to her house."

255

"She never made it back inside at least. Remember Ronnie Lester had gambling debts and was already abusing alcohol pretty badly."

"Was it someone he owed money to sending him a message?" she asks.

"He was paranoid and not thinking straight, the way most addicts not in recovery do."

"*He* did it?" she says.

"In a way," I say. "He told Ralphie that bad people were trying to hurt them. Asked him to help him guard the house and not to let anyone in. Ralphie is like an obsessive guard dog over his family and his home, a crime-stopping caped crusader—probably dressed as Zorro. I don't know if he was asleep and heard something or if he was already in the yard walking the perimeter, but here comes this car with no lights on creeping down the driveway. And he has a sword. He collects them. All of his canes have swords in them. I saw him threaten to pull one on Ronnie the other night when he attacked Dad. But like I say, he could've been dressed as Zorro and the sword was just part of the costume. The sword would explain why there was no physical evidence. He didn't even get in the car. And why there was so much blood and why the cuts and stabs nicked and scraped bone. There's no way to know what's inside Ralphie's mind—he may have thought Janet was working for the bad guys—but I don't think he realized it was her until it was too late."

"Oh my God," she says. "The poor kid. Poor Janet, of course, and her poor mother, but *fuck*, poor Ralphie too. If you're right."

"I think either Verna woke up to check on Ralphie and found him gone or he came and got her, but I don't think Ronnie ever knew anything about it."

"Really?"

"Yeah, and I'll get to why in a minute. I think Verna was utterly devastated and in shock and . . . realizing there was nothing she could do about losing one of her children, began to work to make sure she didn't lose them both. She grabs a blanket and a tent and wraps up Janet and all her things. I noticed a lot of true crime books in their collection—and whether they are hers or Ronnie's, she had seen somewhere in one of them at some point what a rape-murder kit looks like so she makes one from stuff she can gather up quickly in the house. She then puts something down on the seats and drives the car out to a secluded spot on property they own, and with Ralph's help digs a grave and buries Janet. She then drives to a field out on 71 on the way to the party and abandons the car, tossing the rape-murder bag, which now has a smear of Janet's blood on it, into the woods nearby."

"Maybe," she says. "I mean it fits, I guess, but . . . I don't know. Why don't you think Ronnie was involved—in the cover-up if nothing else?"

"Two reasons. The old truck that was stolen."

"The what?"

"The old farm truck that was stolen from a farm not far from where Janet's car was found."

"Oh, yeah."

"When I first heard about it, I thought maybe Janet faked her death and stole the truck to get away, but . . . it was found in town. I think Verna and Ralphie used it to get home after leaving Janet's car. If Ronnie had been involved, he could have followed in another car and given them a ride home. In fact . . . remember the sheets of plastic found up close to the interstate? I think that's what Verna used to sit on to drive Janet's car. I think Verna was taking them home to destroy them and tossed them in the back of the truck when they stole it, but they blew out on their way home."

"Wow," she says, shaking her head. "Wow. It all fits. What's the second reason you think Ronnie's not involved?"

"He wanted to sell the property. Verna didn't want him to, but—"

"What property?"

"The property the new high school is on. He wanted to sell it back in 2000, but she didn't want him to. She had to let him just so they could survive, but that meant she had to move Janet's remains. If he had buried Janet out there with her, he'd've known why they couldn't sell it."

She nods. "That makes—"

My phone vibrates and I answer it.

Someone is already talking before I say hello. Two people. Maybe three. Their voices aren't directly up to the receiver. It sounds like someone butt-dialed me, but then I hear Verna pleading with Ralphie and realize she's called me on purpose.

"Ralphie," she's saying. "Listen to Mommy. Sheriff Jack is our friend. Don't you remember? He's a crime stopper like you."

I put the call on speaker so Darlene can hear it and kick the gas pedal, wondering if the last conversation I'd had with Dad would be *the* last.

Chapter Fifty-three

Janet now had her bottle of liquid relaxer and was back in her car wondering if she should start drinking some now or wait 'til she got to the party.

She didn't want to be drunk. She had never been drunk. She had only drank twice before and just a little beer both times. So she was an amateur drinker who didn't know what she was doing. She didn't want to drink so little it had no effect nor too much so that she didn't remember every detail. How much was that?

As she sat there trying to decide, she suddenly became aware that someone was staring at her.

She turned to see the weird, wild-eyed guy in the VW gazing at her and it gave her the creeps.

Luckily, Little Larry was there. That made her feel safer, but it still unnerved her. And it wasn't that he was looking. She got looked at a lot. Most young girls did. It was the way he was looking . . . totally weirded out and creepy.

She cranked her car and pulled away from the pumps.

Forget him. Think about Ben. Think about how amazing it's

going to be.

As she pulled up to the highway thinking about making love with Ben, picturing it in her mind, she realized she forgot the lingerie she bought just for the occasion.

Shit. Sneaking out in the dark, she didn't even see it on the end of her bed.

Should I go back? I'm already running late.

You have to. Every single thing about this weekend has been too perfect for this, the most important part of it, not to be to.

Nodding to herself, she turned right, back toward town and her house, instead of left toward the party.

Wonder how it's going to feel? Will it hurt at first?

She knew Ben would be gentle.

Would she bleed? How much?

She had forgotten the lingerie somehow, but not the blanket for them to use. It was in the backseat waiting. Waiting . . . like she had been, like they had been. She hoped her mom wouldn't miss it, because she didn't plan on returning it. It was going to be beneath them during their first time and she planned on keeping it forever. Wanted to be able to wrap herself in it anytime she felt sad or lonely.

The night was dark. No moon or stars visible.

She had driven faster than she should have through town, but as she approached her driveway, she slowed down drastically and cut her lights.

Rolling down her window so she could hear how loud her car was on the drive, she listened to the popping and crunching of the little white rocks beneath her tires.

The drive was long and wooded, her car louder than she would have liked, but she couldn't go any slower than she was going. It was just going to take a little while. There was nothing to be done about that.

It's okay. Ben will wait. And I will make it worth his wait.

As she neared the house, she decided to park and walk the rest of the way.

Who was she kidding? She wasn't going to walk, she was going to run.

So it'd be quicker and quieter.

But as she pushed up the gearshift into Park, she heard something.

Footsteps? Rushing toward her? She didn't see anyone.

The sound of someone rushing toward her stopped abruptly, and then she heard another sound. Metal? Metal sliding on . . . what? More metal?

In the fraction of a second before she felt the first cut, she recognized the sound she had heard so many times before. It was Ralphie's sword being drawn from his cane.

Chapter Fifty-four

Quickly but quietly we enter the house, moving through the foyer and living room to a spot in the kitchen where we can hide behind the island and see into the den.

Ronnie Lester is on the floor, his throat so severely slit he looks nearly decapitated, a pool of blood expanding around him.

Dad is seated on the couch, Ralphie behind him with a sword held to his throat.

Verna stands between Ronnie's body and Ralphie, pleading for Dad's life.

We're too far away and there's too little of Ralphie showing and there are too many objects in the way for a clean shot.

"Please, baby," Verna is saying. "Listen to Mama."

"I'm not Baby. I'm Batman."

Like before, Ralphie has his Batman costume on and the handle of the sword he's holding to Dad's throat has a silver bat for a handle.

"You know Sheriff Jack. He's our friend. He's a crime-stopper fighter like you."

Ralphie shakes his head, seemingly confused.

"Trust Batmom," she says. "I wouldn't lie to Batman. Not to my own son. Please put down the Batsword."

The entire scene is sad and surreal, a sickly old man sitting on a couch, a fat Batman in a homemade costume standing behind him holding a sword to his throat, a desperate mother pleading with her son for the life of her former lover, her husband dead on the floor not far from her.

"Any ideas?" I whisper to Darlene.

"Can you make the shot?" she asks.

I shake my head. "No. Not with a handgun."

"I can."

"Are you sure?"

"I've won the state law enforcement marksman competition three years in a row."

"For real?"

"I'm very good."

"Tell you what. Take aim but don't shoot unless it looks like he's about to actually use the sword. Okay?"

She nods.

"That's my dad. Don't shoot him. Don't take the shot unless you have to. Don't take it unless you have it clean."

"I won't. What're you gonna do?"

"Try something else. I'll be back in a second."

When I return a few minutes later, I'm wearing Ralphie's Iron Man costume.

"I'm gonna see if I can talk him away from Dad. I'll do my best to stay out of the way of your shot. If I fail and

263

he starts to attack, go for the shoulder of his sword hand."

"You look ridiculous," she says.

"Thanks."

"It just might work."

"About to find out."

I stand and walk around the left side of the island and stay to the left side of the doorway as I approach, trying to leave Darlene with a clean shot.

As I get close to the entryway to the den, I say, "Batman, Iron Man needs your help. Intruders are breaching the perimeter. Come with me. Do not harm Sheriff Jack. We need his help."

I feel like a prize idiot, but am giving it all I've got, not giving in to embarrassment or self-consciousness.

"Batman, did you hear me? I need your help. Why are you doing that to Sheriff Jack, the newest member of the Justice League? We need him."

"You're not in the Justice League," Ralphie says. "You're an Avenger."

Oh shit. Think fast.

"But you and Sheriff Jack are. The Avengers need your help. Please Batman. Bring your Batsword and come help me with the . . . the Joker. The Joker is outside. He's the one who confused your mind with his potion. He's the one who has you holding a fellow crime fighter like Sheriff Jack."

"The damn Joker," Ralphie says, starting to lower the sword. "I should've known. Sorry about that, Sheriff Jack."

"It's okay. It's not you. It's that damn Joker."

As Ralphie removes the sword and Dad stands up, Verna bursts into tears and collapses onto the floor near the dead body of her husband.

Chapter Fifty-five

While Darlene sits with Ralphie in his bedroom, Verna, Dad, and I talk in the living room.

They are seated on the couch. I'm in a chair across from them. We appear to be the first people to ever actually use the room.

Verna is crying softly.

Through the open doorway to the den I can see Ronnie's body on the floor.

"We've got to call the sheriff's department," I say, "but I wanted to give y'all a chance to talk first."

Verna says, "Thank you."

Dad looks at me and nods.

Verna looks up and over at Dad. "I'm so sorry, Jack. For everything. I . . . I just couldn't lose . . . both my babies."

"I know," Dad says, then looks over at me again. "I know. Nothing we wouldn't do for our kids. I just wish you could've told me."

"I tried. I really did. More than once. I think I had about worked up my nerve and then you were gone, and . . ."

"I'm so sorry I left the way I did," he says.

He had done it for his child, had given up on the case and a real chance for happiness with Verna for Nancy.

"I always told myself if anyone was arrested, I'd come forward and . . . I'd like to think I would have, but . . . I can't be sure. There is nothing in this world worse than losing a child . . . except losing two."

"I understand what you did and why," Dad says. "I really do. And I'm gonna help you and Ralphie in every way I can. And your answer won't change that, so tell me the truth. I really want to know. Did you get involved with me so I wouldn't arrest you or Ralphie?"

"Oh, Jack, no. Of course not. I genuinely, sincerely fell in love with you. I still am. It was all real. Every . . . everything. You saved me. You . . ."

"How were you able to do it?" I ask.

"Whatta you . . . I don't understand."

"How could you even function after it happened? How could you do what you did?"

"It was the hardest thing I've ever done. Several times along the way I didn't think I was gonna be able to do it. I really didn't. I probably stopped half a dozen times or more, but . . . something got me through, something . . . I knew he didn't mean to do it. I knew it was an accident, an unimaginable, horrible, and terrible tragic accident. I knew there was nothing I could do for her. I also knew—and this is what really got me through—she would have done the exact same thing for him. The exact same thing. She adored him and . . . the exact same thing. Still . . . it was so . . . hard to . . . the most difficult thing by far—even more difficult than burying my baby in that cold ground—was . . . getting in that car with her . . . body . . . and . . . driving out to the property. I made it a game with Ralphie. That was hard too. Had him hide in the trunk. He . . . I made sure he never saw her. He hid in the trunk, then dug the hole for me, then hid in the trunk again while I buried her. I protected him and took care of her the best I could. I couldn't lose them both and . . . there's no doubt in my mind—not a single bit in all these years—that Janet would have . . . not just approved but insisted on what I did."

"How many people has Ralphie killed over the years?" I ask.

She hesitates a moment. "Two. Well, three now, counting Ronnie. But he was protecting me. And he thought he was protecting me with all three. He didn't intentionally or willfully murder anybody. Not his sister. He adored her. He . . . I don't even think he knows he did it. He may. I can't be certain. But I think he stuck that sword in that dark car . . . never realizing it was . . . her. He's only mentioned that night a few times over the years . . . and he's never mentioned Janet. He's . . . he only talks about protecting the family and the adventure he had in the trunk. I don't think he's ever associated her disappearance with what happened that night. And not the transient girl who came up on us when we were burying Janet in the memorial garden. It happened so fast. She was on something. Jumped out of the bushes yelling something. Ralphie pulled out his sword as he was turning. He struck her before he even knew who it was or what she was doing. I told him she would be fine. He slept in the car while I . . . did what I did . . . to make it look like a hit and run. He's never mentioned it again. I don't think he knows he . . . killed either one

of them. My crime was covering it up. Just like I had with
Janet. If I hadn't done it when he killed Janet, that poor
girl would still be alive, but . . . after he had already done it,
after she was dead, I . . . just . . . There was nothing I could
do for her. I . . . I used the . . . tractor I had stolen to move
Janet . . . to make it look like a hit-and-run. It's so . . . mon-
strous. I'm such a . . . horrible person, but Ralphie's all I
have in the world."

Dad and I both nod.

"What do you think will happen to him?" she says.

"We'll make sure he's taken care of," Dad says. "Get
him in a good, safe place that specializes in . . . this sort of
thing. You'll be able to visit."

"I'll be in prison," she says.

I try to process everything Verna has said, trying to suss
out the truth, trying to empathize and understand.

"Do you believe her?" I ask.

Dad nods. "I do."

We are standing out in front of the house so we can
talk in private.

Dad looks far older and far more frail than I ever
thought I'd see. He looks conflicted too, his demeanor a
complex mixture of relief and sadness.

"I get it," he adds. "I really do. I'd do the same for
any of you."

I know he means me, Jake, and Nancy.

I nod. "But . . . what she did with the tractor to the
poor girl at the monument," I say.

He nods. "I know. But she did that to a corpse, a . . .
to someone it was too late for. I know Verna, know her . . .

heart. Two times in her life she's covered up what were tragic accidents for her only living child—an impaired child she has to do everything for. Think about how much easier her life would've been if she'd've let him be arrested."

I think about it.

"I love her," he says. "Never stopped. Love her even more now. I want to be with her. Plan to be . . . for whatever time either of us has left—even if it's just a few hours each weekend during visitation in whatever prison she's in, but . . . I . . . wish it wouldn't come to that. Can you think of a way it doesn't have to?"

I think about it.

"Are you absolutely sure?" I ask. "You have no reservations? No—"

"None. I'm sure. Please help her, please help us. Can you think of a way we can . . ."

I think I have an idea, and though I'm less certain about everything than he is, I trust him, his judgement, his integrity. And even if I didn't, or even if I question the clarity of his thinking on this, how can I not do all I can for the man who has done so much for me, for the woman he loves, and for the short future they have together after too many decades of lives far less fulfilled and happy than they might have been?

Eventually, Glenn, his lead investigator, his crime scene officer, and other deputies arrive.

I pull him aside and explain everything to him.

"I've got a favor to ask and a deal to make," I say.

"I'm listening," he says.

"First, there's no way Ralphie is competent to stand trial."

"True."

"I'm assuming your facility can't accommodate someone in his condition and that he'll be sent to Florida State Hospital in Chattahoochee for a period of evaluation."

He nods.

"Would you recommend probation to the state's attorney's office for Verna? Since Ralphie can't stand trial, I don't want to see her treated more harshly than she should. She's lost so much, suffered so much. All she did was try to protect her son, to keep him with her."

"She committed at least three felonies, John."

"Sure. Accessory after the fact. Perjury. Aiding and abetting. Probably others, but . . . given the circumstances . . . given her motivations."

"I don't know," he says. "We're talking a lot of wasted law enforcement time and taxpayer money. Think about the other cases we might have solved, the other services we could have provided. I have to think about all sides of . . . everything."

Everything, I wonder, *or mainly just what voters will think?*

"Here's the deal I'll offer," I say. "If you recommend probation for Verna, she will cooperate, give a full statement—without that you have nothing. You can't get anything from Ralphie. She's all you have. She'll give you a full confession and Dad and I will not say anything to anyone. Not the media. Not FDLE. Not the state's attorney. Our involvement will be invisible. You and your department will get all the credit for closing a very old cold case. I'll say it again. Verna will cooperate fully, make it easy on you, on everybody. Otherwise you have no case. *And* we won't press charges or make public your brother's two assaults on Dad."

The other parts of the deal may or may not have been swaying him, but this last one gets him. His expression and posture and entire demeanor change.

"You worry too much, John," he says. "I got this. Leave it with me. I'll take care of everything. We're talkin' an old lady and a retard after all. I've got to arrest them and take them into custody tonight. He'll be sent to Florida State Hospital. She'll spend one night in jail and have First Appearance in the morning at nine and bond out shortly after that. My guess is she'll get ten years of probation, but she can ask to have it dropped after five if she has no violations. She'll be able to visit Ralphie in Chattahoochee. It's all gonna be okay."

Chapter Fifty-six

Days pass. Then a few more.

It takes a few weeks for everything to settle down and get worked out, but nearly everything worked out as we hoped it would.

The sun is setting on the backside of the cypress and pines across Lake Julia, afternoon receding, evening expanding.

The smell of charcoal and smoked food fills the air.

Dad and Verna sit on one side of our back porch, Anna and I on the other. Johanna is asleep in Dad's lap, Taylor in Verna's.

"We can put them down," Anna offers again. "Are you sure they're not too much—"

"Just a little longer," Verna says. "Please."

Dad smiles and nods.

He looks tired and weak but as happy as I've seen him since . . . I can't ever remember seeing him this happy before.

He is undergoing treatment for leukemia and it's going well. His chances are good for a complete recovery—a safe bet given the way Verna takes care of him.

The state's attorney's office agreed to probation, but she only got five years, and it will probably drop off in two. She moved out of Marianna, leaving behind all the bad memories and ghosts there, and now lives with Dad in Pottersville. They visit Ralphie twice a week and Janet's grave at least that many, and life for both of them is better than it has been in many decades.

"This is so nice," Verna says. "Thanks for having us over as often as y'all do. Nothing in the world beats holding these little girls."

"Our pleasure," Anna says. "We love having you."

When Anna sips her drink or talks with her hands, her new engagement ring catches the light, its glinting presence a source of utter happiness and a reminder that we need to set a date.

"It's ironic," Verna adds, looking out over the lake. "But I feel exonerated. I feel like y'all's investigation and my guilt that it uncovered actually released me from a prison I had been in for a very long time."

"I know the feeling well," Dad says.

"We all do in one way or another," Anna says, reaching over and taking my hand.

As I take her hand I rub her ring, as I often do these days, touching the unending circle, the outward and visible sign of an inward and spiritual grace.

As good as things are in this moment, and they are very, very good, they're about to get better. In a few minutes the food will be ready and Merrill and his new girlfriend, who to Anna's disappointment is not Zadie Smith, will arrive with his mom's special banana pudding for desert, and we will break bread and fellowship and share far more than just a meal. We will participate in a sacred, ancient ritual that is nothing less than a celebration of life itself. For even in all its complexities and difficulties, its small triumphs and devastating tragedies, its scarcity and brevity, life remains worthy of appreciating and celebrating.

CPSIA information can be obtained
at www.ICGtesting.com
Printed in the USA
LVOW12*1440210317
527962LV00005B/73/P